SKYDANCE

SKYDANCE

Book 1

Eli Bertley

ISBN: 1507612702
ISBN 13: 9781507612705

Humanity stands at the edge of Earth. What was once sacred has fallen to ruin. Society, now decadent and depraved, embraces animal instinct, discarding traditions and reason. Buried within indulgence, the light of consciousness now is traded for destruction. The world for sale has become small and barren, leaving only a few reprieves of natural, majestic beauty on the mechanized globe. Ancient secrets are purged by the fast-paced movement of the moment. Countries are gone; the only entities left are totalitarian corporate monopolies controlling what viable resources remain. As the wealthy terraform the planet for their masters, people in the pits of barrio slums are indistinguishable. Covered in sweat and tar, they build barriers meant to keep out those deemed undesirable. Slaves to progress, none have time to contemplate life or enjoy the dreams that are sapped away by the first sign of daylight.

The future has always been uncharted territory dancing in the back of each generation's consciousness. Society evolves in many forms, bridging science fiction and science fact. Mindless livestock commute to individualized meat grinders. Cars drive themselves, hovering just above the road. Technology is a beast, opening doors and eluding the great divide on the red horizon. If life had an emotion, it would be, at best, irony. Mental piracy hijacks reason as knowledge is no longer learned but injected into the brain during childhood. The globe has been broken into zones scattered across all continents and monitored by an intensely meticulous group known as the Watchers, cyborgs whose brains are connected to a web of machines. They see everything and quash nearly all forms of resistance to the world order, tasking vast numbers of pitiless enforcement brigades with crushing the very notion that it is possible to rise up against the system. Each day brings unique assembly to keep an individual self. Nothing sacred and nothing taboo, the mechanized world of tomorrow is a rustic global ghetto for self-indulgence and power. Maintaining a single entity is impossible, yet a spark does remain from a lost world and a time long forgotten: the Awakening.

The Etharchs came from the heavens one day, and like most things from the dark recesses of space, they dazed and bewildered the masses as they laid out their ground rules: "We will have control either by conquest or consent." Afterward, they acquired another name, the Watchers. They treated the rich like pets, lavishing them with imaginary power as they forced the rest of humanity to transform the world into an environment more suitable for them. As a consolation prize, the Etharchs gave humans the Skrying. Considered a blessing by some and a curse by the rest, the Skrying holds the only truth left untarnished and private in a world where everything is controlled and monitored from every angle: the genetic marker that couples every person on the planet.

Thirteen years after birth, a sensor inside each person activates, calling out to its match, of which there is only one, belonging to the individual's soulmate. Each sigil pair is unique in size, color, and appearance, yet all resemble a key. They ensure that everyone on Earth is inescapably marked and accounted for. Once the two keys activate, both humans are imprinted with a love for each other that only the heavens could tear apart. No matter one's status or where one lives on Earth, the power of the sigil pairing is irrevocable.

Chapter 1

It is a night drenched with rain. A man runs through alleyways, dragging his young son behind him as if malevolent, unseen forces are at their heels. "There's nothing to fear, Zeke," he says to his frightened boy. "Your time will come, and all will be well." He pushes the bewildered child into a small crevice in an alley. The man stands alone as spotlights capture him. He makes his final stand against them, crying out, "You may have seized me, but you'll never stop the truth and those who believe as I do!" He races toward the lights, shouting before everything goes white.

Ezekiel shoots straight up before the alarm goes off. Haunting dreams of the past have been resurfacing more and more lately. He slumps to the kitchen, waving his hand over the coffeemaker before hopping into the shower to prepare for another day. As the coffee wakes him up, he stares out the window at the frenzied chaos of people racing to and fro, trying to survive the city streets, which lie in wait, always hungering for the weakest person to slip up and feed them.

Ezekiel struggles to keep hope, as he has since the moment an idea first bloomed in his head: If you could change the stars, would you? If you had foresight of things to come, would you redirect their path? Would you stand up against mysticism and tyranny if given the choice? He always laments over the stories of yesterday, stories of how beautiful and simple life once was. Stories of a time when humans weren't fugitives on their own planet or slaves to an unyielding system of spies and tyrants. Still, he is one of the lucky ones. While most toil at the very bottom of the system, he is as close to the top as one can get without crossing over. Force barriers keep the lines divided, demarcating two classes of society.

Ezekiel works as a mechanic, mostly on the vehicles of the elite. He is also known to dabble in law enforcement, the province of the Cons. An artificial cybernetic intelligence force, the Cons were designed to keep both societal classes in line and to dispense the Etharchs' justice. They are judges and executioners at a moment's notice. Most are the size of regular humans, but others can tower over small buildings.

The toll of working seventeen hours a day doesn't seem to weaken Ezekiel's morale. He plugs away, hoping he might someday change his stars. He figures that if he saves up enough money, he can buy his way into a better life. The constant work also keeps him from dreaming about the future too much.

Walking home at the end of the day, bypassing the usual symphony of chaos, he realizes he must have worked longer than usual, considering that one of the only two forms of entertainment for the wretched masses is about to take place. A panoramic screen hovering above the street bursts to life with a flamboyant announcer greeting all viewers, riling them up in anticipation of the night's show. "Welcome, all, to another eventful evening! It's time once again for *Elysian Runner*! As always, I'm your host, Malthus. Tonight we have a real show in store for you, so let's bring out our contestants!"

Ezekiel pauses to catch a glimpse of the disgusting display about to unfurl. More a lesson in obedience than a show, *Elysian Runner*'s premise is to pit men and women against freakish beasts in a fight to the death. The beasts are the work of the Etharchs, who sometimes mix species to create monstrous creatures straight out of ancient mythology. Always a massacre, the spectacle gets its title from its contestants, who often run in terror, screaming for heaven to take them before the beasts do.

"Tonight we have for you a defiler of our way of life. He was found defacing statues with messages that called for war and anarchic revolution." Into the stadium walks a terrified boy no more than twelve years old. Heading toward the center of the arena, he stops in front a weathered statue of a blind woman holding a pair of scales in one hand and a sword in the other, a relic of centuries past. At the base of the statue are assorted weapons. He picks a trident from the eclectic collection and gazes at the other end of the arena. Down a blackened corridor, a monster from nightmares is about to be unleashed. "Let the games start!"

The stadium lights dim until only the boy is lit, standing on sand that is soaked in coagulated blood. A growling, rumbling noise from the opposite end of the arena grabs his attention as three sets of yellow eyes peer out from the shadows.

Trembling in terror, the young lad stands his ground, trying not to show fear. Light suddenly fills the area, illuminating the Cerberus, a three-headed dog the size of a boulder with a snake for a tail. "My, my," says the announcer. "It seems that man's best friend will be playing tonight. They certainly outdid themselves with this one. Let's see how long it will be before this defiler is ushered to the Fields."

Unable to move, the young boy stands frozen as the beast slowly moves in for the kill. Then in an instant the creature leaps into the air, pouncing onto the boy, who screams as the flesh is quickly torn from his body.

"Oh, what a shame! This one seemed to have promise. But not to worry, we have many more exciting matches tonight, so don't go anywhere. We'll be right back after a word from our benevolent leaders."

The screen fades into propaganda as Vincent Avarice appears. In addition to being president and high councilor of all ruling companies, Avarice is the head of Liquidation, the company that controls the planet's water, and the chairman of DIRE Industries, which manufactures the Cons. Always polished and well-groomed, Avarice is a natural-born politician. He has a particular gift for public speeches, turning words of treachery and corrosion into messages of empowerment and necessity. "It has been nearly three centuries since humanity was saved by the Etharchs," he says. "When they arrived, they found Earth dying after a third world war, with limited resources to care for an overpopulated planet. They rescued our ancestors from the brink of extinction and gave them a renewed sense of purpose and the possibility of a future brighter than any of us could have imagined. Join us for the tercentennial celebration of our saviors in the weeks ahead."

Easily pulling himself away from the primal, barbaric amusement, Ezekiel comes across a beggar in an alley being beaten by several men. "Hey!" he yells, but they pay him no attention as they continue their vicious onslaught, pummeling the man to the ground. One of the thugs raises a fist to finish the assault when Ezekiel intervenes, knocking the assailant to the concrete. He quickly regains his footing, and now all the thugs focus their attention on Ezekiel.

"Why don't you all just go on and we can call it a night?" Ezekiel says. The thugs pause for a moment before ganging up on him. As the vagabond watches, Ezekiel takes them out one by one. Defeated, they scamper into the night as Ezekiel walks over to the beggar to see if he is all right. Leaning over to check on him, Ezekiel is blindsided as the victim delivers a moderately deep cut to his forearm before running the same way as his attackers.

"That's the thanks I get for putting my nose where it doesn't belong," Ezekiel says, walking back onto the main street. Peering around the corner, the hobo looks on with glowing blue eyes.

Needing a drink after his failed attempt at chivalry and the brutal display of *Elysian Runner,* Ezekiel heads down to the Evening Land, a watering hole soaked in enough liquid indulgences to steal away all inhibitions. Pushing past the depraved madmen in the throes of panduesas (euphoric female companions available to anyone with lusts that need satisfying), he sits down at the bar and orders a triple shot of whiskey. Staring off into space, focusing on his Skrying, he's suddenly interrupted by a voice: "Careful. Keep that pace up and I'll have to save you from an onslaught of duesas."

Ezekiel snaps out of his reverie and looks over to see Cesare Etebari sitting down beside him.

"Take it the day was long?" says Cesare.

"No more than usual. Just thinking about that boy in the Running."

"Yeah, rough way to go at that age for some graffiti, huh? Still, better than when they did that woman for trying to hand out that crazy literature several weeks back. You remember that? Wendigos ripping her apart, body parts flying left and right. Still can't for the life of me understand why they feel the need to give some of those creatures such high intelligence just to torture and devour us."

"Same reason they only sent out three instead of twelve or more: to make a statement," Ezekiel says.

"I guess. But still, man-eating humans? No thanks. I would rather have the Cerberus."

"Could be worse," Ezekiel says. "They could make us watch it sober."

"And how are my two favorite bar patrons doing tonight?" says Lexi, kissing and squeezing Cesare and nodding to Ezekiel. She is a panduesas and a philium, an Etharch-human hybrid: a beautiful per-version of two worlds. She has infused herself with amphibian traits for display; genetic modifications are common among the mysterious panduesas.

"You're looking quite lovely this evening. How's business?" asks Cesare.

"Like always. They prefer one or the other, never care for half-breeds," she sighs.

"Then that's their loss, to turn away a unique and rare beauty such as yourself."

Lexi blushes in embarrassment, her skin darkening from a translucent sea green to shades of indigo and rouge.

"Why don't you find another line of work, then?" Ezekiel asks, trying to break up the flirtation.

"Because it's even harder for a girl with no allegiances to either side to find legitimate work," she says.

"That really sucks for ya. It truly breaks my heart."

At Ezekiel's cold words, Lexi's body turns a bright yellow before Cesare puts a calming hand on her shoulder. Slowly returning to her original color, Lexi says, "You two gentlemen have a good night. I'll see you later, sweets." And with that she slinks away, allowing her tail to caress Cesare before whacking Ezekiel on the head.

When she's out of earshot, Cesare turns on Ezekiel. "Why you got to be so hard on her, Zeke? She's a nice girl. It's not her fault what happened to her. What would you do if Etharchs accosted your mother and you were the result? She tries to be nice, but you just won't give her a chance."

Ezekiel sighs heavily. "Look, I don't have anything against her; she's all right in my book. Besides, you've never heeded my advice about the stables of women you hook up with anyway. I'm just trying to save both of you from heartache. What's going to happen when your Skrying activates and you imprint on some other female? How do you think she'll feel when that happens and she's left all alone because she doesn't have a Skry?"

Cesare's heart sinks at Ezekiel's words, which he knows are true. Hybrids can't Skry or imprint, which doesn't leave Lexi many options for love or financial stability.

Later on, completely drunk and out of money, the two stumble out of Evening Land and into the dimly lit streets, heading toward home. Cesare keeps bumping into Ezekiel as he takes swigs from a bottle of brandy. "You think it will happen to us?" Cesare asks. "Skrying,

I mean? Maybe we're among the lucky few who won't imprint. After all, it's been seventeen years, and ours haven't even been activated. Maybe our matches are dead, and we should live life to the fullest."

"Perhaps," Ezekiel says thoughtfully. "But I won't take that chance. Besides, you're the only person I need in my life, amigo."

"I hate to have to imprint on your ugly face," Cesare retorts, spilling the remains of his bottle and inciting both of them to drunken laughter.

Finally making it to his place, Ezekiel promises to see Cesare the next day and watches him stumble away toward home. He heads up to his own apartment in the massive building that houses the working half of the city. Ezekiel ponders the words of his lifelong friend. Cesare is the only one he can trust after experiencing his mother's execution and the spectacle of his father's death at such an early age. He and Cesare are more like brothers than friends, relying on each other to survive. But, he thinks, what if Cesare is right? What if they've missed their awakenings? It isn't uncommon for mates to be torn apart in this mad world, whether by violence or opposing political views. Sometimes there are also what the Echelon and Etharchs call convergence breeches, where two people from the two different classes find each other and imprint, causing mass hysteria and upsetting both the upper side and the Off-World Order.

As his body slowly succumbs to sleep, Ezekiel wonders if there is someone out there truly meant for him.

Chapter 2

"We are children of a star, waiting to be acknowledged as loyalists. Our forefathers and every generation since have had an ironclad deal with the Etharchs, amassing untold wealth and securing our survival."

Vincent Avarice says this to his fellow elitists, who have come together in the standing beacon in Zone One. "If anything, at least we will all be spared to continue our species. They've held up their end of the bargain for centuries, and now that they're about to achieve what they've been planning, what else can we do? It's too late."

"It's never too late. We still have a chance to warn everyone." This from Ahriman Bushyasta, the president of Siphon, the company that controls Earth's air quality and distribution.

A dry voice from the conference room doorway rises like a whisper. "It seems we have come at an opportune moment in this discussion of yours."

"Lord Ambassador Adramelech, I wasn't…we weren't expecting you here tonight," Avarice says, trying not to tremble.

A cloaked figure looms over the room, piercing, soulless eyes staring out of his pale face. "Well, one does like to respond to gossip and

accusations; it eases any minds that might stray into foolish thinking."
He strides into the room. "Yes, it is too late for any of you to back out
or rebel. Let me make it clear: you are a means to an end, nothing
more. The fact that you acknowledge this is precisely why we chose
you. You will be rewarded, not sacrificed like your planet or the rest
of your species. The mass extinction of your insignificant kind will
happen shortly after the tercentennial, when we will take over as the
sole inhabitants of this world."

"What about the uprisers or Origen? Will they be a threat?"
Bushyasta asks.

"Soon our work will be done, and when that happens, it won't
matter what those simple creatures have planned, because they will
be dead," Adramelech responds.

"How do we know you won't just dispose of us once you're done
with your plan? What's to stop us from overthrowing you before that
happens?" Bushyasta demands.

Before anyone can move, Adramelech reaches out and snaps
Bushyasta's neck with a quick motion of his wrist. Bushyasta's head
twists around a full 360 degrees before thudding onto the conference table. "You don't. I grow weary of idiotic questions. Serve us
diligently, loyally, and we will see that you and yours are well taken
care of. Fail and suffer the fate of the rest of your people." With these
words, the ambassador departs as quickly as he arrived.

In stunned silence, each Echelon head departs to their transport-
ers, which will send them back to their home zones. Before leaving,
Lilith Myriad, president of the land and food distribution company
Deracinate, pulls Avarice aside. "Do you really think they'll hold up
their end of their bargain and keep our families safe?" she asks.

"What choice do we have?" he responds sharply. "Just do as you're
told."

Arriving home, Avarice greets his wife, Rachael, with an empty kiss. "Where is Serenity?" he asks.

"Upstairs in her room," Rachael responds feebly.

Avarice opens the door to his daughter's room to find her sitting by the window, amused by the floating orbs that are dancing above her head. "They say when two lovers die, their souls dance in the stars as they head toward the heavens. I like that idea," says Serenity. She turns around to gaze at her father with engaging hazel eyes.

"If that is what you choose to believe, darling, go right ahead. You know I don't put much thought into fantastical nonsense." At his response the light leaves her eyes, and she turns back to her orbs.

The girl hasn't imprinted on anyone yet, a fact Avarice takes comfort in. It means her virtue is still intact, and he can continue to fool himself into thinking his genocidal work will preserve her. Keeping her from harm and stopping anyone from tainting her beauty, which he relishes, is his only objective. He even insists she use her mother's maiden name instead of his, to shield her from any potential harm that might befall her as the daughter of the very person bent on bringing about mankind's downfall.

Realizing the severity of his words, Avarice rushes to say, "Serenity, you are my only joy, the only decent thing remaining of myself. You have tethered my soul in place."

She smiles faintly but says nothing. At a loss, he leaves and quietly shuts the door as she starts to sing an old hymn her mother sang to her as a child.

⚏⚏

The glow of a distant fire pierces the faded sky, signaling a new day. At the hovercraft plant, the repetitive tasks of his job leave Ezekiel more lethargic than when he first woke up. He's in another world until the sound of a wailing man halts production. Ezekiel cuts through a growing crowd of his coworkers to find the source of the screams:

a man whose right arm has been sliced off, the result of a machine malfunction. The man collapses to the concrete, his body convulsing in seizures before it eventually goes still, having bled out.

A loud boom shatters the ghastly scene, catching everyone off guard. Explosions start to ripple on the far side of the factory, heading in their general direction. Workers make a mad dash for the nearest exit. Sprinting for his life, Ezekiel dodges falling debris while vaulting over crashing obstacles and fallen people. As he escapes from the plant, not daring to look back, a final explosion catapults him through the air and throws him to the ground. After slowly picking himself back up, he turns to look at his workplace, which is now little more than a bonfire. The uncertainty of what might happen next has him fleeing the scene before the Cons arrive. Without thinking, he quickly heads toward Evening Land, but before he can go very far, he's jerked into an alleyway by the same men he'd stopped the other night.

"Well, it's always good to see familiar faces. I guess you all didn't learn the other night," he says as fists fly at him, knocking him to the ground. The gang thrashes him mercilessly before one of them screams in fright. Before Ezekiel knows what's happening, they're running away as fast as they can. Bewildered, he turns around to see the same homeless man he'd helped before. "I take it you want to finish what you started as well?" he says, trying to catch his breath.

The grimy man leans forward. "The time is almost at hand," he says into Ezekiel's ear. He makes another quick incision in Ezekiel's forearm. "To help others find you and guide the way of my brothers." Holding his arm in pain, Ezekiel looks up to question the reasoning behind the crazy homeless man, but the man has vanished yet again.

Eventually, Ezekiel saunters into Evening Land, hoping to remedy the wailing that's still ringing in his head, as well as the sharp pain in his arm. He notices that the place is consumed by silence. All the patrons' eyes are firmly fixed on the holographic display screen above the bar, watching the tragedy unfolding at the plant before it cuts to a live feed of Vincent Avarice.

"Citizens of Zone One, a great atrocity has taken place today. The terrorist group known as Origen has destroyed the hovercraft plant, which helps this great city flourish and provides transportation and jobs for the less fortunate. The number of fatalities hasn't been tallied yet, but we know there were almost no survivors. Let me make one thing clear: we are a strong society. We will find these seditious criminals, and they will answer for their barbarism. The wise zone leaders have talked to our great saviors. While they are saddened by this atrocity, they believe justice will prevail. Even though the journey to healing hasn't begun yet, confidence in the knowledge of our imminent recovery brings light to this darkened day. Any information on Origen member whereabouts will be rewarded."

Ezekiel wonders how they could have known Origen was behind the attacks so quickly, yet been unable to stop them in the first place. As he ponders this, a voice interrupts his thoughts.

"Zeke, thank goodness you're all right! I was just about to contact Cesare to see if he had heard anything about you. I'll let him know you're OK." Lexi is squeezing his arm, elated to see him still among the living.

"Appreciate the sentiment. After this incident, I might have to join you and start scraping by for a living." He pointedly removes her hand from his arm. Lexi smiles disappointedly before leaving him to his devices.

"Barista, double shot of Venom," he says. The bartender slides a double shot of whiskey mixed with synthetic snake venom toward him. The drink brings on a feeling of hallucinogenic lucidity, clearing the mind of rubbish (at a great cost to dexterity) for several hours. Slamming it down, Ezekiel zones out to the chatter of the other bar patrons, who can't stop discussing the destruction of the hovercraft plant and Avarice's speech.

Unlike the rest, Ezekiel is more interested in the meaning behind all the insanity that has been swirling around these past few months. Origen has been attacking with ferocity recently, as if they know something is coming. Unseen by the rest of the sheep-like masses, they consider themselves harbingers of a time before Skrying and Etharchs, claiming that the knowledge they hold would make everyone think differently of their "saviors from space." They portray themselves as selfless vigilantes trying to preserve humanity and a way of life without any help from Off-Worlders, but their actions only fan the anger of those completely brainwashed by the system.

As Ezekiel ruminates, the Venom starts to take hold, pushing everything else away and swiftly carrying his mind to otherworldly realms. He closes his eyes, focusing solely on the trip. A flash of dark sapphire flashes in his mind's eye. Swirling like a cyclone over water, a chaotic vision slowly comes into focus. Violence sweeps across the land. People scream as fires rage. One by one, the faces of the Etharchs rise up until they reach a diamond floating in the sky. The diamond pulsates with light, shining down like a beacon. Everyone left on Earth falls down motionless. A vision of children laughing and playing replaces the perplexing images for a moment before a flash of cerulean light washes everything away. Slowly the light recedes to reveal a pair of hazel eyes, staring as if they are trying to see directly into Ezekiel's soul.

Ezekiel snaps back to reality, sitting up to familiar surroundings.

"Looks like you hit the stuff a little too hard last night, my friend," Cesare says.

Regaining his senses, Ezekiel realizes he's in Cesare's apartment. "How did I get here?" he asks.

"No need to thank me. It was the least I could do," says Lexi with a smirk. She slinks by Ezekiel in a silk apron that clings to her body.

"Say what you will about her, Zeke, but she's a true humanitarian in more ways than one." Cesare smiles as he watches Lexi walking into the bathroom, her tail swinging happily. "I'm glad you're all right, amigo. Thought you were toast for sure after the bombings yesterday."

"Bombings? I thought it was only the plant that was hit." Ezekiel still feels groggy and subdued.

"Well, after your little bender at the bar, there was an attack on the DIRE plant as well. The Elitists are apparently more upset about that one than the factory, even though there were no casualties. None so far, anyway." Cesare hands him a cold glass of water.

"So they hit both the auto plant and the Con plant? Sounds like a busy day," Ezekiel says.

"Well, not to worry," Cesare responds. "The bigwigs are cleaning up the streets right now. They're arresting all suspicious vagrants and citizens, to ease everyone's minds. Safe to say you might want to stay here for a while. They were asking a lot of questions about you at the Evening Land after Lexi brought you here."

Lexi emerges from the bathroom. "Hey, babe, I've got to get back to work. Got to pay the bills till you make an honest woman out of me."

Cesare smiles, but it's with a heavy heart. Their eyes meet for a moment before she blows him kiss and walks out the door.

Cesare turns his attention back to Ezekiel. With a grin he says, "So, buddy, what do you want to do today, seeing as how you're now officially unemployed?"

Ezekiel decides he'd rather ponder his current predicament alone and tells Cesare he's heading to the Sanctuary. One of a handful of remnants of untouched land, the Sanctuary has been preserved for centuries as a sort of new age botanical garden. The area teems with exotic greenery and wildlife, all flown in expressly to occupy the government-sanctioned ecosystem. Besides functioning as a preserve, the Sanctuary provides natural resources to citizens in every zone. It is one of the few places where one can get close to seeing what the world was like before the war and before the Etharchs.

Walking for a bit, Ezekiel spots the place where his parents used to take him as a child. Sitting down near a pond, he basks in this rare moment of solitude. The familiar locale prompts him to think about his past, and all the unanswered questions about his childhood: Why were his parents sentenced to die? What made them so dangerous to the establishment that the small acts of defiance they committed incurred such a harsh punishment?

Just as he's fixing to leave, he gazes over the pond and beholds a woman he's never seen before. She has the radiance of a sapphire. Her skin glows white as milk, while her amber hair dances in the breeze, concealing her face. He can just make out the sound of her humming. It's a tune that is unfamiliar to him.

He continues to watch as she feeds a school of fish. Suddenly she looks up at him. His heart stops, his eyes transfixed by hers. Time and space hold no meaning in this moment. Her gaze tied to his, bridging the distance between them. Without warning, his arm begins to pulsate. He looks down to see that his Skry is starting to glow neon blue, stronger and brighter than any light he's ever seen. He looks over at the girl to see her staring at her own arm, which is glowing radiantly like the sun as well.

Ezekiel knows what is happening: they're Skrying. He figured his awakening would never happen, that his soulmate was either dead or on the other side of the world, but clearly he was wrong. She stares at him with astonishment and terror, not knowing what to do or make of the situation. Without a word she turns to run away, toward the outer regions of the Sanctuary. He rushes to follow her, then stops himself, remembering the force fields between each section of the ecosystem. He has no way of knowing who she is or where she is going, but at least he knows now that she exists and that they will eventually find each another again. For the first time since he was a child, Ezekiel is happy, believing that maybe his luck is about to change for the better.

Chapter 3

Ezekiel is just about to enter his apartment when the door swings open. A Con pulls him in and throws him onto the couch. He looks around and realizes that his entire apartment is crawling with Cons.

"What's going on here?" he says.

"Sorry for the informality, but you're a hard man to find," a voice responds. Ezekiel looks over to see a man leaning against a wall, smoking a cigarette and then prematurely putting it out on his floor. "Name's Ravana. I'm head of the task force of all Cons. Please excuse the display of force. But considering that no one could find you, and you are one of a handful of employees to survive the terrible attacks that happened the other day, the bosses didn't want to take any chances."

"I don't understand," Ezekiel says.

"It's quite simple. We know the bombing at DIRE was an inside job, and we're questioning all those who are still among the living," Ravana says. "Now, let's pull up your file. Ezekiel Carthage. Ah, I see your parents were executed when you were twelve. Your mother, Sophia Pistis, was arresting for handing out blasphemous literature and resisting the Cons. Your father, Castiel Carthage, was executed in the Running after organizing a militia offshoot of Origen to overthrow the government." He sits down across from Ezekiel. "I remember your father's death. It was one of the best displays I ever seen. He lasted longer than anyone would have expected, fighting his way through several battles before meeting his end at the hands of the Behemoth. Have you ever seen it? The Behemoth, I mean? Not many have. It's only brought out for the special ones. Horrible way to go, but if it makes you feel better, he was dead before he was eaten." Ravana sits back, and the two stare at each other. "So, are you picking up where your parents left off?"

"No, I'm just trying to make an honest living," Ezekiel replies.

"Well, see that you do," Ravana says. "In the meantime, we'll be keeping an eye on you and monitoring your moves until we can prove your innocence." Ravana stands up and the Cons begin to vacate the apartment. "Have a good day now," he says, disappearing out the door and leaving Ezekiel reeling. He sits in silence for long time.

⚞⚟

"Mother, Father, where are you?" Serenity yells, bursting through the door.

"What's wrong, darling?" Rachael says, rushing to her aid in a panic.

"Look, look, it activated!" Serenity says, holding out her glowing arm.

Rachael stares in horror. "When and where did this happen?"

"At the Sanctuary. I saw him across the lake, and we both realized that we'd found each other. I don't know who he is. I've never seen him before."

"What's going on here?" Vincent demands as he enters the room.

"Your daughter—she's Skried!" Rachael exclaims.

Looking down at his daughter's arm, he sees the undeniable truth. "Where? Where did this happen?"

"At the Sanctuary," Serenity answers. "I saw a young man across the lake, and it just lit up and started pulsating. I don't know who he is."

Vincent's brow furrows. He walks away, leaving both women flabbergasted. "Vincent, where are you going?" Rachael calls. But Vincent doesn't respond. Instead he storms into his study and pushes a small button on his desk. Instantly the door locks and the window shades come down, throwing the room into total darkness, except for the light from a glowing sigil in the center of the room. Hesitantly, Vincent walks over to the glowing marker and steps into the center of the room. The sigil glows brighter and pulsates faster and faster until a hologram projection of Adramelech appears. "To what annoyance do we owe this disturbance?" he says.

"My daughter. She has awakened," Vincent says humbly. "Her Skry, it has found the one designed to be with her."

"And is this supposed to concern us?" Adramelech says.

"You told me it was impossible for her to Skry, that you took care of any chance of this happening," Vincent says, an angry note creeping into his voice.

"As we recall, you asked not to be fodder, and to be given leeway when we burn this planet to a cinder, not to make sure your daughter's virtue would remain intact before or after."

Vincent glares defiantly before composing himself. "My lieges," he pleads, "I beg of you. Find out who this person is so that my mind might rest and I might and better serve you."

There is a long moment of silence. "Very well. We will find out who she is Skried to. But Vincent, never bother us with petty, insignificant matters again. Are we clear?"

"Yes, my lord," Vincent responds. The image of Adramelech fades out and light returns to the room, making everything as it was before—everything except Vincent Avarice, who looks around in worry and fear.

⌗⌗

The cold, massive building looms over Ezekiel. He looks up at it as if a mortician's knowledge is buried within its hollow halls. His footsteps echo through the archive cave, where very few come. Most think that the past is better kept in dreams and distant memories, but he can't get what Ravana told him about his parents out of his head. It all happened so fast and at such a young age. Only fragments remain, leaving gaps in his restless mind.

He walks over to an isolated rectangle in the corner of the massive warehouse of history. Standing in front of a pale gray column, he says, "Sophia Pistis." Suddenly an enormous projection appears, surrounding him with news articles and pictures of his mother. He proceeds to watch a newsreel of the arrest:

"*Sophia Pistis, the radical author of* Childhood Lost, *was arrested and contained today. Pistis is a key member of Origen, the radical terrorist group attacking and killing people, seen here inciting violence with hateful speeches that claim the Etharchs are here to conquer the Earth and that our wise and great Echelon leaders are merely puppets meant to secure our compliance. She is scheduled for purification this coming Sunday, the twentieth of April.*"

Ezekiel pauses, allowing what was concealed from him for years to sink in before requesting her execution tape. In earlier years, before *Elysian Runner* became the sole province of executions, there was the Purification Purge. Purification was a ghastly way to exterminate people, mostly women, children, and old men. The condemned were injected with drugs that made them more compliant before they took their place in front of an Echelon tribunal. As the masses watched, their crimes were cited aloud; only then were they painfully executed, as a warning to those who might follow.

Ezekiel watches as his mother is presented before the shadowy, cloaked figures condemning her. They then stand her on a podium and light her on fire. He watches in horror as she stands there as still as a statue, submitting to the fire as if it is a friend. He freezes the footage and zooms in to look into her eyes. They're wild and alive, screaming out with the pain her mouth is unable to voice. Tears slowly creep down his cheeks.

He then asks for the archival news history on his father, Castiel Carthage. He gazes at endless articles and pictures of a rugged man leading refugees against their tyrants. He finds out that his father became a revolutionary shortly after Ezekiel's mother was burned alive. Nothing is mentioned of his life before the uprising. Ezekiel then asks to watch his father's execution, only to be shocked that there wasn't just one but five attempts at killing him. Apparently he even fought off death in *Elysian Running*, fighting heroically against a twenty-foot snake, spiders that spat webs of acid, a pack of wolves that could camouflage themselves like chameleons—even a dragon, no less. However, it was his final fight against the legendary Behemoth that did him in. The fight lasted several minutes, with Castiel limping the entire time. The beast was just too quick and monstrous to beat. It snatched him up and squeezed the life out of him just before devouring him, to the delight of the applauding audience.

Ezekiel's sorrowful tears evaporate into a steam of anger. Knowing that acting on his present thoughts and feelings will only bring about the same fate that befell his parents, Ezekiel crashes through the door to his apartment. He is frustrated by what he saw at the archives and overwhelmed with a surge of emotions that can only cause him trouble.

Ezekiel decides to vent in the only true, peaccful way that will calm his soul and his mind. He rummages through his closet and pulls out a classy vintage tux to wear. Left by his folks, it is his only memento of them. After getting dressed, he looks himself up and down in the mirror before leaving his apartment and heading for the theater.

The Orpheum, a theater that resembles the ancient theaters of old, is the only place besides the Sanctuary where the all of society, the slaves of destitution to power hungry mongrels are almost able to comingle with the Echelon. It also offers the only other form of entertainment allowed to the masses. Barriers of Cons and force fields keep the classes apart as the elite hover above all on the top floors while everyone else is relegated to the ground.

The performance tonight is of a special quality. It is broken up into two acts. The first one is a short musical interlude, while the second is a film of early-twentieth-century origin called *The Great Dictator.* As the overture slowly begins to rise, flutes and brass instruments quietly usher in the sounds of melancholy classical guitars and somber alto saxophones before all gracefully fade into silence, allowing a hauntingly beautiful tune on a lone piano to grace the auditorium.

Ezekiel is entranced by the melody. His mind begins to drift to fond memories of his childhood: being twirled around by his father while his mother watches and smiles from a distance as the three of them enjoy a beautiful day in the Sanctuary. He also remembers something his father once told him: "Truth and courage once guided men like stars. Now power and fear do, while wealth pours in for a few and agony pours out of the rest like blood."

A short intermission is announced snapping him out of his daydream. Ezekiel decides to get some fresh air and accompanies the masses streaming out of the auditorium to relieve and refresh themselves. Walking through the crowd, he manages to slip by the Cons and force field, knowing of a glitch in the field that has been overlooked for years. In his suit, he appears to part of high society. He crosses over from the worn wooden planks downstairs to the black pearl floors upstairs, into rooms adorned with golden garlands and white columns. He walks over to the balcony he frequents every time he goes to the Orpheum. As he leans on the railing and gazes out at the world, his arm starts glowing again. He looks down in puzzlement as the Skry glows brighter by the second. His focus is on his arm when a voice from behind him breaks the silence.

"Well, it's nice to know you have an appreciation for the theater."

He turns around to find Serenity standing in front of him. A flood of knowledge flashes between the two of them. Thoughts and memories of happy moments from each of their lives begin imprinting on each other's consciousness. Rising out of the joy, negative memories also surface, but both remain standing. Only the memories of their parents are left undisclosed.

The entire situation is puzzling to both. Cognitive transfer has never been known to happen during Skrying; pairs simply fixate on each other and are left with the feeling that no matter what happens, the person they're staring at will always be there for them and love them unconditionally. They both gasp in shock.

"That was different," Serenity says. "I wasn't expecting to meet you again so soon."

"Me either. I'm Ezekiel. My friends call me Zeke."

"Nice to finally meet you face to face. I'm Serenity, Serenity Meera. How come I've never seen you here before? I come here often. It's the only place where I can blend in and disappear from everything and everyone."

"Yeah, I know the feeling. I hardly ever have the time. I'm always plugging away working. Usually when I come here it's just to enjoy the view and the open air. I feel like I'm sitting in another world when I look out from this spot."

"I have that feeling too when I'm near the pond where you found me the first time," she says. "So what exactly do you do, if you don't mind me asking?"

"Well, I did work in the Cons and hovercrafts plate until yesterday," he says, losing himself in her dazzling eyes, which are matched only by her endearing smile.

⚏

"He's a what? How can this be? I thought Skrying between the two classes was impossible!" Vincent Avarice says to Adramelech.

"We are just as intrigued and concerned as you are. It is rare that it happens. Usually we know about it before they ever meet and imprint, for obvious reasons."

"You personally assured me she would be protected, that I wouldn't have to worry about her mixing with unfavorable elements," says Vincent. "Now, not only do I find her Skried, but Skried to the offspring of Castiel Carthage! He was a great nuisance in the past and incited such an uprising that we spent much of our energy and time returning things to normal. You had better fix this or—"

"Don't threaten me, mud monkey," Adramelech hisses. "Remember who it was who plucked you from obscurity and gave you keys to the kingdom. We can easily replace you or torture you and your kin before terminating you!"

"Forgive me, my lord. I didn't mean disrespect," Vincent says. "But I must be able to focus, and it is hard with my only daughter, my only child, Skrying to that piece of filth."

"Don't worry, we will take care of him. As for your precious offspring, we have a solution for that as well, one that benefits us all," Adramelech says. "Together, we will keep them apart, and all of this will disappear like a fading memory, just like Castiel Carthage. In the meantime, set in motion the next step in the plans. Bombing the plant was a great success. Now find who was responsible for the other bombing and start the next phase."

⚏

"So you're from the other class? I thought that was impossible. And yet here you are, standing with the elites and Skried to me," Serenity says.

"I don't know about the Skrying, but as for standing here with you, that's easy," Ezekiel says. "I know where there's a short circuit the force field long enough to slide in."

"Don't you think it is fate, that we Skried to one another?"

"I don't know," he says. "All I know is that I think you're the most beautiful thing I've ever laid eyes on. I thought so even before we imprinted. I've found truth now, and it lies in your eyes." She blushes and smiles.

"Ms. Meera? Are you all right?" one of her guards calls to her. "You are missing the show."

"You must go, Zeke," she says. "If they find you, I fear what they might do to you."

"I fear another second without you over death. I must see you again," Ezekiel says.

"You will. Now that we've imprinted, we'll always know where the other one is." She looks down at their brightly glowing forearms.

"I'll see you soon, then," he says. He gazes on her one last time before racing back inside. He's gone just before her guard comes out onto the balcony, asking again if she's all right. Serenity only stares blankly at the spot where Ezekiel last stood.

Ezekiel sprints around corners, hurrying to get to the force field. He thinks he is in the clear before being stopped short by a Con.

"How did you get here?" the Con demands. "How did you get past the force field? You're under arrest!"

Quick on his feet, Ezekiel maneuvers around behind the Con to open the control panel on its back. He disables its primary functions temporarily, just long enough to make his escape. He races toward the force field again. Just as he's passed through it, the Con reboots itself and sounds its built-in alarm, transmitting that there is a breach in the force field. Feeling as if his lungs could explode at any second, Ezekiel dives out of the Orpheum and into the shadows, narrowly avoiding capture as multiple Cons arrive in front of the grand theater.

※

Serenity is ecstatic on returning home. She never thought it was possible to feel the way she does, particularly for someone deemed beneath her and unworthy. She smiles, her mind lingering on his dashing, rugged looks, his wavy, slicked-back hair. She's about to open the door when it opens of its own accord. Her mother is standing in the doorway, a panicked expression on her face.

"Mother, what's wrong? What's the matter?"

"It's your father. He...he found out who you were Skried to," Rachael says.

"How ironic. I just met him at the Orpheum tonight," Serenity says.

"You what? Oh my goodness, don't let your father know. He'll lose his mind." Her mother trembles.

"Why will I lose my mind?" Vincent says, rushing down the stairs.

"My Skry. I met him tonight. He's very sweet," Serenity tells him.

Crimson flashes across Vincent's face. "You what? The hell, you say! No daughter of mine will imprint with trash! In time he won't even be remembered, like his parents!"

"What are you talking about?" Serenity asks. "What do you mean he won't be remembered? And how do you know who his parents are?"

"It doesn't matter. I've taken the necessary precautions. Soon none of this will matter. Everything will be all right, princess. Everything will go back to normal, the way it should be." His voice still shakes with anger. "Now go upstairs. It's time that we all retired."

"No, Dad, I want answers!" Serenity says defiantly. "I'm crazy about him, and I won't let the only decent thing to come into my life get taken away because of your warped thinking!"

In a flash, Vincent slaps her across the face. He keeps slapping her, his temper at a fever pitch, until she flies backward, falling onto the stairs. Rachael rushes to her daughter, grabbing her face in her hands. She wipes away Serenity's tears and the blood trickling from her lower lip. Both of them turn to stare at Vincent in shock.

Vincent is breathing heavily, flecks of spittle on his mouth. Slowly, as he comes to his senses, the look of rage on his face is replaced by one of disgust and shame at the thought of what he has done. "I'm... sorry, but you left me no choice. You will stay away from him. I'll double the guards so that they can keep a constant watch over you until this matter is resolved." He hesitantly embraces his daughter. "Serenity," he says, with lingering anger and determination still in his voice, "I only want you and your mother to be safe."

Serenity nods, knowing there is no point in trying to continue the conversation. She slowly walks up the stairs to her room, afraid to look back at her father. Vincent looks to his wife, who slinks away in terror, leaving him standing alone.

As she gets ready for bed, Serenity's thoughts are still on Zeke and what her father said. What did he mean by "like his parents," and what "necessary precautions" did he take? Her father has never hit her before. What is it about Ezekiel that made him do it? Suddenly, for the first time, she is truly afraid of her father. Afraid of what he is planning not just for Ezekiel, but for her as well.

⧈

The doorknob twists open as Cesare walks into Ezekiel's apartment. "Zeke, you here, buddy?" he calls. There is no response, only the sight of Ezekiel's trashed apartment and an eerie silence. Nothing is intact, not a single trinket left unharmed. Cesare is searching for signs of life when suddenly he finds himself shoved against a wall. He lands with a thud, only to be thrown again onto Ezekiel's overturned coffee table. He's lying on the floor when a voice whispers wetly, "Where is Ezekiel?"

"Sorry, don't know who you're talking about," Cesare says insolently.

A black, spherical shape slithers its way up to his face, hovering a second before plunging its claws into the bone of his forearm. Cesare screams in pain. The creature stands him up roughly before catapulting him into the wall again. In a flash it has its hand around Cesare's throat.

"We want Ezekiel, Mr. Etebari, and we are prepared to do anything to make sure we get him," the creature says, its beady yellow eyes lingering on Cesare's face.

"So you're saying you'll either reward me or punish me if I get in your way, huh? Good to know. If I have some pressing need to become a snitch, I'll just ask around for a wrinkled black salamander."

At his words the creature digs its claws deeper into Cesare's neck before smashing him through the wall. Before Cesare can land, the creature catches him in midair, slamming him headfirst against the floor before returning its hands to his throat once more. "The name is Iblis. You would do well to remember that, and to take my offer seriously. After all, your lady pays her dues by turning tricks. If you helped us, you could put an end to that. Or I could just go pay her a visit and destroy everything you love about that little half-breed." Iblis grins manically as he digs his claws deeper into Cesare's neck, choking off any possible rebuttal. Cesare's face is red with fury.

"We'll be watching," Iblis whispers. "See you soon, monkey." With that he disappears as quickly as he arrived.

Propping himself against a wall, trying to catch his breath, Cesare tries not to think of the deal he was just offered, nor what it might mean for the two people he cared about most in this world.

<hr />

The sheer happiness from meeting Serenity has put hope and happiness in Ezekiel's mind for the first time since he was a child. He can't stop thinking about her. Serenity…she came from nowhere, and now he is trying to figure out how was it possible to live this long without knowing her or feeling this way. He can't wait to tell Cesare about her. Although, Ezekiel thinks, what is Cesare going to think about us being from different classes? He can only imagine his friend's sarcastic response and mocking laughter at the news of the unlikely pairing. Figuring talking to Cesare can wait until the morning, Ezekiel decides to just crash instead, knowing that's probably what Cesare himself is doing anyway.

He makes his way through his sector back to his apartment. He's less than a block away when a loud explosion throws him to the ground. He looks up to see his building engulfed in flames, most of which seem to be emanating from his floor. His charred personal effects rain down from above, comingled with ashes. Unsure whether this is a response to his meeting with Ravana or Serenity, what he does know is that Cons are on the way, and he needs a place to lie low.

⧓

A prism of light appears in the quarters of Vincent Avarice. In the moonlight streaming from the window, smoke from his cigar dances seductively around his hunched silhouette. Suddenly a shadow appears in the doorway: Ravana. The Con pauses, afraid to inform Vincent about recent events. "Sir," he says tentatively, "Mr. Carthage's apartment had been destroyed. There has been no sighting of him at any of his regular hangouts, yet there was no sign that he perished in the explosion either."

Vincent gives no response. At the unsettling quiet, Ravana quietly departs, leaving Vincent to puff even more furiously on his cigar. Suddenly he bolts upright in his chair. He drops his cigar, picks up a glass paperweight, and hurls it across the room. His enraged eyes stare out the window, and embers from his cigar land on his beard and singe it.

⧓

Ezekiel's knock echoes on the metallic door. Minutes seem to pass as he waits anxiously, only to be greeted by the barrel of an AK-47 aimed right between his eyes. "If no one answers you the first time, that's usually a sign to piss off," says a voice from behind the gun.

"Always glad to see you, Samson," says Ezekiel.

"Zeke?" says the voice. The gun is lowered for a second, only to be returned to its original position. "What makes you think my offer to put a hole through you is off the table?" Samson says.

"I'm sorry. Look, do you think we could do this inside? I'm in a lot of trouble, and I'm desperate for your help, man."

Samson lowers the gun again and waves Ezekiel in before shutting the door behind him. Trinkets and pictures of wars past welcome him into the cramped living quarters, along with a plethora of weapons ranging from the sleekest cutlery to the most exotic guns. Everything is nestled securely on Samson's quaint barge, bobbing up and down on what is left of the ocean. Samson himself is a testament to an old life, looking as if he belongs in a history museum. Tall and strong, he's as tough as steel and as deadly as the end of a knife. Always wearing a black beanie to cover his mane, he sports a shapely beard that elongates his face.

"How's business been treating you?" Ezekiel asks.

"Hanging in there. Would've been better if I hadn't decided to take those excuses for parts off of you," Samson retorts.

"Come on, man, how was I supposed to know what you had in store for them? It's not like you told me you were going to build a mobile bomb out of a Con. All you said was 'Hey, do you think you could smuggle me out some Con pieces?' They have authorization codes that have to be inputted before they're operational."

"Yeah, well, when a short-circuiting police officer blows up right before it reaches its destination point, and then dives headfirst into a street cleaner, that doesn't look too good for my credibility, bro. Do you know what people have been saying lately? They say, 'Hey, Samson, you're really cleaning up the streets. We're sure to put an end to this tyrannical mess with you on the job.'"

"I'm sorry, I—"

Samson cuts Ezekiel off with a wave of his hand. "What kind of trouble you in now?" he asks.

Ezekiel tells him about Serenity—meeting her at the Sanctuary and again at the Orpheum, how he Skried to her, that she's an elite. He also tells him about being chased by Cons, and that his apartment has been reduced to a ball of fire. When he finishes, Samson nods thoughtfully. "Wow, sounds like a hot date," he quips. "At least your life has become a little more interesting. You can stay here for the night so long as you don't mess with my business. I don't need any of your issues raining down on me. If you feel the need to go out, don't get tracked back here."

"Thanks, man, appreciate it," Ezekiel says.

As Samson walks away to continue his work, Ezekiel glances at a mechanized suit called a RAMBAM. "And don't touch Lailah, shes my prized possession. It's not every day you can get the opportunity to hollow out an industrial size Con meant for defense and make it a battle suit." Samson yells over his shoulder. "Plus I Don't need you sinking my home."

Chapter 4

Everything is cold and black. From the edges of opposing peripherals, two stars move toward one another, leaving a trail of light that looks like a rain of sparks, falling a short distance before fading out. Arriving in the center, the stars dance in perfect harmony but never touch each other. One's color alternates between champagne white and neon turquoise, while the other burns a soft, fluctuating cerulean. The pace of the dance begins to pick up until the stars form a circle of turquoise and cerulean, exploding the darkness with a burst of light.

Ezekiel wakes to Samson banging away at his work. The intensity of his dreams of late has left him holding on only to Serenity's face to keep his sanity.

Walking over to pour a cup of coffee, he watches Samson putting his own coffee cup down with his left hand and lifting a bottle of Scotch with his right, shaking it as if to ask if Ezekiel wants any. "No thanks, think I'll let you enjoy," he says as Samson's hands move back to working on the machine gun he's melding with a flamethrower.

Ezekiel sips his coffee and zones out for several seconds. Suddenly something snaps him to attention. He's filled with the sensation that something may be wrong with Serenity—that he needs to get to her right away. He also realizes that Cesare is probably freaking out, wondering if Ezekiel's dead or alive. Ezekiel decides that since it's on the way, he'll make a quick stop at Cesare's to ease his friend's mind. Without a word he proceeds to get dressed.

"Hey, I'm going to go check on Cesare to let him know I'm still alive," he tells Samson. "I'll tell him you got uglier since he saw you last." He smiles, but Samson only responds with a finger gesture of annoyance.

***

Serenity's eyes open. She's moving slowly today. Her head is still pounding from last night's fight with her father. She had the same vague dream that Ezekiel had. Not knowing what the dream could symbolize, she decides to just freshen up and not focus on the throbbing pain she feels.

When she looks in the mirror, she sees red welts giving way to black and blue bruises. She splashes water onto her face and reaches for a topical cream on the counter. She gently applies a generous amount, replaces the cap, and looks at herself in the mirror again. She watches as the swelling and bruises vanish instantly, along with the pain. With a deep breath, she prepares to welcome the onslaught of a new day, but her thoughts dwell on Ezekiel. Even though he's just appeared in her life, she feels as if she's known him forever. Will she ever see him again?

***

Ezekiel knocks on Cesare's door, only to have Lexi open it in a flurry. "Zeke, you're alive! I heard about your place. Thank goodness you're all right. I've been worried all night about you and Cesare."

"He never came home?" Zeke says.

"No, I haven't heard from him since earlier yesterday. You don't think he was there when your place blew, do you?" Overwhelming worry is written on her face.

Ezekiel just stands there in silence, thinking over what she's just said. "I'm sure he is just fine. Don't worry, I'll go find him."

"Zeke, please be careful," she warns. "Your face is everywhere. They're saying you're part of the resistance and that you're considered extremely dangerous. There's a price on your head, nearly five hundred thousand currencies."

He doesn't respond to this. He only gives her a deep hug and immediately goes on his way.

Cautiously making his way through the slums, he grabs a worn hooded coat from a stand in the marketplace, keeping alert for Cons and Cesare until he walks by titan screens outside the identification processing building. His face is on all of the screens. Above his head are the words "Wanted for terrorism and conspiracy to commit terrorism. Reward if still breathing five hundred thousand." Ezekiel stares for a moment. Quickly regaining his senses, he turns and bumps into a lady, who catches a glimpse at his face. He brushes by her, trying to remain calm, only to hear from behind, "It's him, the terrorist!"

Activity in the market comes to a grinding halt. The patrol fixes on his position as he makes a dash for a side alley with the Cons right on his tail. Pounding his feet against the pavement, he leaps up onto a garbage can, jumping to grab hold of a ladder that is attached to stairs that lead to the top of a decaying building. He begins climbing higher and higher. Below, the Cons lock in on him and set their weapons to stun. Before they can shoot, he dives through a broken window headfirst, rolling a few times before regaining his feet. As he sprints down a long hall full of disposed items, broken glass, and half pillars, shots whiz by his head. The Cons have entered the building and are right behind him. He spots an exit just as a direct shot lands on his left side, paralyzing his arm and causing him to stumble into a wall. He's dazed for an instant but then jumps to his feet again, flinging a nearby door open and dragging himself up a set of stairs. Finally making it to the roof, he barricades the door with a discarded pipe as he tries to figure out what to do next. Flying by at an opportune time is a large hologram billboard. Gathering his courage, he dashes toward the edge of the building, leaping with all his might. The Cons bust through the door only to see him soaring in midair. He smashes into the side of the billboard, grabbing hold of the hologram's maintenance frame and holding on for dear life.

Using all his energy, he's able to pull himself up onto the billboard's platform. He turns around to see the squad barreling through the air and landing perfectly right beside him. One of them swings a forceful arm into the frame, barely missing him. The blow causes a part of the scaffold to break off and plummet to the street below. Ezekiel breaks off another piece of the frame with his intact arm and wings it at the Con's feet, sending it falling to the far-off ground. Before he can regain his composure, two more swoop in to capture him. Using his body as a ram, Ezekiel lunges to the left while swinging the metallic club at one Con's head. At the blow it goes flying into the hologram, short-circuiting both the screen and the remaining Cons. Bystanders below watch in amazement as the ongoing combat gliding above them shoots out sparks in every direction. Soon the Cons are dropping to the earth as well, causing panic among the pedestrians lining the street. Gazing at the chaos beneath him, Ezekiel returns his attention to finding somewhere to jump off when a single Con climbs down from the top of the billboard. Before it can move in and attempt an arrest, another bolt of electricity ensnares it. The Con explodes, setting off a chain reaction that leaves the entire billboard engulfed in flames.

Ezekiel braces himself for a crash when he sees an approaching building. He takes a deep breath and jumps, crashing onto the roof.

He looks back and watches the hologram billboard crash into the identification processing building, exploding on impact. A large crowd of people stares in shock at the pillar of flames swallowing the building. In minutes, citizens and government officials run screaming from the building just before it collapses.

Knowing air units are already en route, he runs for the stairs. He decides to find Cesare and Serenity later and instead heads for the only place around he knows is safe.

Chapter 5

Along with the remaining corporate heads, Avarice looks over schematics of the plans in store for the citizens of all the zones. As he examines the plans, he smoothly delegates tasks to each head with a smile. "Newly elected President Hiro Mokushiroku of Siphon, you are in charge of air filtration and general air quality. Your job will be to remove clean oxygen from the air while blocking the harmful pollutants and releasing them back to Earth. I will take charge of disinformation, assuring the public there's nothing to worry about while we finish gathering viable water supplies and desalinating the oceans. Thetan Haram, you will be given a third of the Con forces to keep any retaliators in line, as well as to round up all livestock and vegetation in the growing sectors. Tristan Van Chieu, you will inform all elites about the details of their guaranteed safe passage. Your job is to divide those who will survive from those who will perish with the rest of the unfortunates when the celebration—"

Suddenly Ravana walks in, interrupting the meeting to quietly inform Avarice of a situation in the slums. Avarice rises to his feet. "That will be all for now, gentlemen," he says. "I have some urgent issues to attend to." He and Ravana hurriedly exit the boardroom.

Entering Avarice's private office, Ravana divulges the full details of what has transpired. "Say that again?" Avarice asks, a note of incredulity in his voice. "The processing building is what?"

"Gone, sir. Apparently some Cons were in pursuit of Mr. Carthage and chased him onto one of our flying billboards. A fight ensued, with the result being that both the enforcers and the vessel itself crashed into the side of the building and exploded. It's now showing on all manner of media. The spinoff is—"

"A spinoff? Who authorized that?" Avarice interrupts furiously. "Do you know what this will look like to the Etharchs? They'll assume we're ill equipped to handle this situation ourselves."

Before Ravana can apologize, a hologram of Adramelech appears. "So this is what you consider containment of pests? Did we overestimate your ability to handle things when we put you in charge, Avarice?"

"No, sir, containment measures for this incident are in the works as we speak. We're also crafting a spinoff story to keep the lesser unaware of the—"

"I don't care about your pathetic excuses and attempts to quell the sniveling insect masses! Do the job assigned to you or we will find someone who can, leaving you and your family to wallow and gnash your teeth with all the other doomed souls."

The hologram disconnects. Avarice looks over to Ravana, glowering at him. "Find this nuisance now or I will have you processed!" he exclaims, and Ravana nods hesitantly.

⁂

Serenity watches the unfolding events in astonishment. The reports say that a violent and dangerous rebel leader destroyed the processing building. Ezekiel's face is plastered on the screen. She can't believe it. How could she be Skried to a man capable of committing such atrocities? Her mother, Rachael, sits beside her, holding her hand the entire time.

"Oh darling," Rachael says, "I'm so sorry this is happening to you. Your father is figuring everything out. Rest assured, this madman will be caught soon and condemned, leaving you free of the burden of being Skried to him. Then it will all be simply a nightmare to be forgotten." She says this to try to comfort her daughter, but Serenity doesn't know what upsets her more: the fact that she has fallen for a vigilante, or what her mother says will happen to him now. She jerks her hand away, leaving the couch and the reports, and begins walking toward the door.

"Where do you think you're going?" her mother asks frantically.

"I'm going to the Sanctuary. I need to be alone and clear my head, Mother," Serenity answers.

"I don't think now is the best time, dear. Why don't you and I go sit by the pool and drink a little bit and relax?"

"Because drinking and running away from the facts of what's happening won't help us, Mother. It never does," Serenity says.

"Look, sweetheart, I know things haven't always been easy for you, what with your father being who he is and you having to live a secluded life. But we do it to protect you and to ensure your safety from those who would…" Rachael falls silent.

"Who would what? Kill me? Use me to as leverage over Father? Put an end to our cushy lifestyle while the rest live in death and misery?"

Rachael just stands there in silence, hanging her head at the truth her daughter has spoken. Serenity immediately knows she has spoken harshly. It's unfair to attack her mom when her father is truly the one to blame. "I'm sorry, I didn't mean to take it out on you. I'll be back shortly. I just…I just need to be alone somewhere I feel comfortable." Serenity turns and walks out the door.

A series of pounds calls Samson to the door. When he opens it, he finds a tired and battered Ezekiel standing there. "Get in here," he says, looking around suspiciously to see if Ezekiel was followed. "Well, that was one hell of a walkabout you had yourself this morning," he adds.

"Cons were on me and didn't leave me any choice," Ezekiel says.

"I saw it like everyone else did. At least you've provided some entertainment to go with my work for the past couple of hours. And really pissed off the whole lot of the Echelon." Samson smiles. "Time for a drink." He brings out a huge bottle of whiskey and two glasses, filling both equally until the whiskey almost spills over. "To the dangerous rebel who would destroy peace and tranquility in the slums of Zone One, bringer of chaos on humble civil servants and pets alike: a toast. I give you aged whiskey, Momma's own recipe." His humorous toast completed, Samson inhales his entire glass before immediately pouring another one.

"Cesare never made it home last night," Ezekiel says in a monotone voice. "I think he went to see me at my place before..."

"Don't worry, he's a tough dog. I'm sure he is fine. Probably more worried about you at this point, Mr. Half-a-Million-Currency Man. Not too shabby."

"Thanks for not handing me to the wolves," Ezekiel says.

Samson waves him off again. "You're family. Even though we've had our differences in the past, that's not going to change anything. Besides, you're hardly lacking in the amusement department. It's not every day an old friend has a bounty put on his head, with Vincent Avarice personally fronting the cash. Plus I'm curious how much I can really get if I hold out a little bit longer, given the rate of your daily outings."

They both laugh at this and continue to drink their whiskey. "You know," Ezekiel says, staring to feel the booze, "the three of us are all we've really had. I mean, you had something of an upbringing, but the truth is, you, Cesare, and I have only really had each other, especially these past couple of years."

"I forgot, you get all emotional when you start to drink," Samson says, taking Ezekiel's glass from him.

"Seriously, though, when things get rough, where do we turn?" Ezekiel says.

Samson considers the question. "Well, Cesare has Lexi. You have the bottle, which we share joint custody of. And I like to think my work keeps me going." He continues slugging back drink after drink.

"But this girl, Samson, she's unlike anyone I've ever met."

"Of course not. She's from the upper side of this hellhole we live in," Samson replies.

"No, it's not that. I mean, yes, she is from the Echelon, but it's more than that. Regardless of the Skry or all the other factors, I feel like I've known her for a thousand years." Ezekiel starts to doze off as the wheels in his brain begin to turn.

"Well, good on you, man," Samson says. "At least now you and Cesare will be less likely to come barging through my door asking me bail to you out yet again."

A couple of hours go by. Once Ezekiel feels the coast is clear enough, he decides to head back out in search for Serenity and Cesare. He can't stop thinking about Serenity and can't shake the notion she's in trouble. Taking a few supplies, he slips off of the barge, leaving a passed-out Samson lying in his hammock. Standing outside of the boat, he looks up to see that the night sky is clear for the first time he can remember. He doesn't have a clue where to start, but he has an idea and only has to be close enough to set off the Skry.

What is left of the decimated moon shimmers on the water, illuminating the grass caressing Serenity's feet. She's sitting in the place where she first met Ezekiel, pondering everything that has recently transpired. Can love truly exist for her within all this madness and turmoil? Is it her path to wander alone, yearning for the love of a radical she can never hold or touch? She looks down to see her arm glowing. Her Skry is signaling that he is near. She looks around, hoping to catch a glimpse of him, and immediately spots him right across the pond where they first saw each other.

From his side of the pond, Ezekiel stares hopelessly, lost in the vision of loveliness that has stolen his heart and robbed him of his senses. Holding up his hand in a wave is the only gesture he can think to make. Serenity stands up to walk closer to him but stops at the edge of the grass, knowing there's no way she can get to him or him to her. Both linger in silence, unable to speak. Then Ezekiel starts to feel a strange sensation, a feeling unlike anything he's ever felt before. His Skry is pulsing once again, with the pace picking up speed by the minute. Serenity watches from a distance as her own Skry starts to pulse with the same pattern, shining a brighter and brighter shade of radiance. He looks at her again, and in that instant, a bright, condensed light shoots forth from his hand across the pond, hitting the invisible force field. Speechless, she shoots the exact same beam from her hand to collide with the barrier.

As the beams of light start to grow in intensity, Ezekiel and Serenity notice the electrical wall is beginning to short out, flickering and twisting in the light until a final pulse from the two shoots forth and destroys the field altogether. Unable to comprehend what has just happened, they stand frozen in bewilderment. Ezekiel rushes toward the water and dives in. Clearing the pond in seconds, he stands up, soaked, in front of Serenity. "Fancy meeting you here," he says.

"Somehow I figured you would find me here. What was that?" she asks.

"I don't know," he says. "I've never seen anything like that before. I came to make sure you were safe. Something told me to come find you and check on you. I also wanted to tell you that I'm not a rebel. The Cons came after me. They blew up my apartment, and now they're forcing me to run for my life." He pauses for a moment, and then continues. "I know you don't truly know me, and you don't have to believe anything I say. But I had to tell you the truth and make sure no harm had come to you."

Their eyes are caught in an unbreakable stare, stopping time. Sirens start to go off in the distance, but they're unable to break their bond. "We have to get out of here before they come and arrest you," she says. "If they catch you, they'll execute you." Smiling, he grabs her by the hand, pulling her to his side as they run into the night.

⁂

Swinging back to consciousness, a disoriented Samson falls to the ground, trying to get up with sea legs. After achieving a vertical stance, he starts calling out for Ezekiel for a few seconds before he realizes he isn't there. "Crazy, persistent fool," he mutters. Just then there's a knock at the door. "Yeah, coming," he yells, walking toward the door. He opens it to find Iblis looming above him, a soulless smile piercing his face.

⁂

"So this is how the other side lives. How do you do it?" Serenity asks Ezekiel.

"Usually you don't sleep in," he says.

"I knew from what I've been told that it's hard living, but I never imagined it was this disheartening," she says.

"True, we all live minute to minute usually, but somehow you feel more alive, more appreciative of what you got, because you know it could be worse. Let me show you." He cautiously leads her past a half-standing building. On each floor there are residents inhabiting the available space, all exposed to the street below. "Some are fortunate to live in places like this. A community emerges from different species, genders, and creeds, all protecting one another from the ravenous cannibals or roving gangs that prey on the weak and destitute in this city. Or you can end up in Origen, fighting the 'good fight,' which has been going on for what seems like forever." He turns to her and sees that his words have made the light in her eyes go dim. He pulls her into a comforting embrace and smiles. "It's getting late. Let's head to the safe house, where we can see someone in a worse predicament than the one these people are in."

A few blocks down and around the corner, they're brought to a standstill by the sight of Samson's boat engulfed in flames. In horror, Ezekiel mutters Samson's name under his breath.

"What do we do now?" Serenity asks.

Ezekiel just stands there for a moment before snapping to attention. Knowing of one other place they can hide, at least for the night, he takes her by the hand and says, "Come on."

⊶⊷

"Find her!" Avarice screams, his voice echoing through his mansion. "I don't care what you have to do, what stones you have to overturn, or whom you have to torture. Just find her!" His servants scatter frantically, leaving only one person in front of him: his wife, Rachael. "This is entirely your fault!" he shouts, slapping her to the ground. He grabs her by the hair and pulls her into the foyer. Her screams and his strikes are the only sound resonating throughout the cold manor.

⊶⊷

Ezekiel scours the block, looking for any signs of life. He returns to a spot where he told Serenity to stay put until he could make sure the coast was clear. "Come on," he says, "I know a place up ahead where we can stay for the night." He gently takes her by the hand, and the two of them walk up to an abandoned, half-demolished church on the outskirts of the city. They gingerly maneuver through falling scaffolds and support beams to get inside. As they walk past rotting pews toward the altar, Serenity glances at the symbols all over the dilapidated building, symbols whose meanings have vanished from thought and history.

Taking her into a partially exposed office on the left side of the former vestibule, he grabs a couple of blankets and throws them around her.

"How do you know about this place?" she asks.

"My parents told me stories of what it was like back in their parents' lifetime. How communities would go to places like this and socialize. They showed it to me right before they died. As kids, when Cesare and I would cause mischief for the Cons, we would run to this place to hide, knowing no one would ever think to look for us here. It's been a long time since anyone came to cathedrals like this. Ever since the Etharchs arrived, everyone thought it was pointless, I guess."

She snuggles up next to him. He looks down at her, a little taken back. "I'm cold," she says, and he puts his arm around her. After a few minutes, she begins to fall asleep on his chest.

"Tomorrow we'll find some food. After that, we'll stay here a couple more days until it's safe, then we'll head over to another friend's house. I only hope they're OK." He says this out loud to himself as she peacefully dozes on him.

Never in his lifetime would he have believed the past several days could have happened, at least not to him. He caresses her head, moving away the hair that covers her face. He looks down on what he believes is the most beautiful thing he's ever seen, then drifts off to sleep.

Several hours later, Ezekiel is awoken by a rustling noise out in the main area. He delicately repositions Serenity on a broken piece of furniture so he can go investigate the noise. He walks out, prepared for anything, but finds nothing. The sound of fluttering in the rafters makes him look up, but there is nothing but creatures of the night moving on to some other roosting place. Realizing his mind is playing tricks on him, he returns to the warmth of Serenity and quickly falls asleep again. A creature too smart to be seen watches closely as the two rest peacefully, unaware they are being observed. In the darkness, its glowing blue eyes are the only things visible.

When Serenity awakens the next morning, Ezekiel is nowhere to be found. She calls out his name in a panic, wondering what has happened to him. Has he gotten captured? She starts to hyperventilate in fear when she hears him calling her name. She gasps before running to Ezekiel, who's carrying some food he got for breakfast. She nearly knocks him over with the force of her embrace.

"I see you're a morning person," he says, caught off guard by her intensity.

"I woke up and you weren't here! I didn't know if the Cons or something else had taken you, or worse."

"Hey, it takes a lot more than Cons to catch me, let alone kill me. Besides, I figured you might be hungry, so I opted for takeout from a close friend in this part of town." They sit down to eat the food he has brought. The food isn't up to the standards Serenity is used to. It isn't moldy or rotten, but it is very basic. She knows it's expensive to get food and other resources to the slums, but she always thought places like the registration centers and other government subsidiaries took care of such things. Seeing more of what life is truly like on the other side, she begins to lose her appetite. "I'm sorry about your friend," she says. "Things were crazy last night, and I didn't get a chance to say it."

Ezekiel stops gorging on his breakfast. "Thanks. He was a great guy. Rough around the edges, but I believe you two would have gotten along."

"So what's next for us, considering that the place you originally planned to take us isn't there anymore?" she asks.

"I have one other place we can go, but I think we should wait until nightfall so we have better cover," he says before returning to his meal.

Engines whirling above their heads stop them from further food and conversation. Ezekiel grabs her and they run to the center of the church, crouching behind a pew and waiting in silence. He peeks over the top to see a patrol group of Cons drop down through the roof and begin to circle them.

"What are we going to do?" Serenity whispers.

Ezekiel forms a plan as the Cons climb over the rubble and start scanning the area for any signs of life. "I guess your old man is smarter than I gave him credit for," he says. "OK, follow my lead and stay behind me." He picks up a heavy piece of ceiling that has fallen to the ground. He leaps up over the pew and swings in midair, sending one Con flying backward into an exposed pillar, cracking its sternum. "Let's go!" he says, grabbing her as the rest of the Cons spot them and start shooting.

Ducking and dodging the Cons' shots, Ezekiel and Serenity run out the side of the building toward the harbor. With the Cons hot on their trail, they leap without thinking into the water as bullets fire in their direction. After diving into a pipe for cover, they swim for several feet before finally making it to a pocket of air. They lift their heads out of the water, gasping for breath.

"Are you OK?" Ezekiel asks.

"Yeah, just trying to get used to all this. Where are we going now? It's so cold."

He makes his way past her to scan the area for other avenues of escape. "I guess it can't wait any longer. We hang out here for a little bit, and when the coast is clear, we'll make our way across town, lying low before heading to my friend's place. I just hope your father or his employees don't find us there."

What seems like hours float by as the two uniting hearts shiver in the icy waters. Discovering a manhole, Ezekiel climbs up to look around, searching for any sign of life from the robotic police canvassing every sector for them.

"The coast is clear," he shouts down to her, reaching out a hand to help her up.

"Where to now?" Serenity asks. She's shivering and completely drenched. Staying close behind Ezekiel, she follows him over to a closing shop. "Excuse me," Ezekiel says to the shopkeeper, "I don't suppose you'd mind giving us something dry to wear?"

The shopkeeper recognizes Ezekiel from the news updates and the wanted holo-projecting stones. He immediately freaks out and runs away, screaming, "The terrorists are robbing me!"

Ezekiel starts laughing. He looks over at Serenity, who's giving him a penetrating look. "What? He was going to say that anyway. Why make him a liar?" he says. Serenity keeps giving him the same look until his smile disappears entirely.

After changing their clothes, they race toward the only place Ezekiel believes will be safe at this point. Knowing what is waiting when they get there, and what's in store if they stay out on the streets, he decides to cut through a deadened forest. Hollowed, withered trees dot what was once a park, now riddled with ghostly memories of innocence lost.

"Where are we?" she asks.

"Used to be a park where we all congregated when we were younger. Over time the planet has become more punishing and less forgiving to us all. That's why the Sanctuaries are so vital. They're the only place now where trees grow and fresh, drinkable water flows." He says this as they pass by a meadow of dirt. The moonlight cuts through the smog, shining a clear beam in front of Serenity and causing her to stop. After going forward several feet, Ezekiel turns around to see her step into the light. Immediately little bursts of light start popping out of the ground.

Stunned, he slowly walks up to her as the blips of light start moving about her as if in a dance. "The light is moving," she says, "almost like it's calling out to any and all who are holding light to show themselves." He joins her in the beam of light. Standing together, their eyes lock in a lovers' stare as a sudden explosion of specks of flying light pop up.

"They're fireflies," Ezekiel says, mesmerized. "I didn't think they could survive outside the ecosystem." He looks over at her, hypnotized by her smile. He reaches out a hand and brushes her hair from her cheeks. Serenity begins to tremble with anticipation of a kiss long overdue. As he begins to attempt to kiss her, the fireflies erupt beginning to twirl around them, encasing the two in a soft cyclone of light that spirals up to the sky. Ezekiel pulls away realizing how exposed they really were "Come on" he says. Together they watch the light show fly up and disappear into the night sky.

⧎

"Zeke, you have more grace with you than the stars in the sky!" Lexi says, rushing to hug him.

"Sorry, this was the only safe place I could think of. Do you mind?" Ezekiel asks.

"Are you really asking if you're imposing? Of course not! You know me. Nowadays I'm either out working or at Cesare's. Make yourselves at home." Lexi smiles. Her small apartment resembles a rundown version of the Sanctuary, cluttered with various enchanted plants. "And who's this lovely lady?" she asks.

"This is Serenity, my Skry," he says, showing his glowing forearm as proof.

"Well, it's certainly a pleasure. I never would've thought I'd see the day when you would Skry. I guess that leaves Cesare alone to deal with li'l old me."

"Speaking of Cesare, I can't find him," Ezekiel says. "Were you able to finally get a hold of him?"

Lexi's smile disappears. She points to the other room without saying a word. Ezekiel makes his way around the flora and fauna to see Cesare sitting quietly in a corner of the kitchen, his face bruised and swollen.

"What the hell happened? Who did this to you?" Ezekiel exclaims.

"Some flunky for the Etharchs. Goes by the name of Iblis. I went by your place the other night to check in on you, and when I got there this thing was waiting for me, thinking I was you. He grilled me for a while, made some threats, but I didn't say a word. They blew up your place, man. Sorry."

"I know, man. It doesn't matter. It's just good to see you alive," Ezekiel says.

"We are heading over to his place, Zeke, so feel free to stay as long as you need to. Just contact us by way of underground channels, love." Lexi helps Cesare up from his chair, and Ezekiel hugs him hard, glad to know he's still alive. Lexi and Cesare depart, leaving Serenity and Ezekiel alone.

Silence now engulfs the apartment. Tranquility finally surges over the pair. Imminent danger is held at bay, at least for the moment. Not knowing where to go from here, Ezekiel and Serenity sit awkwardly across one another. Barely acquaintances, all they know of each other is what they were designed to know. They're from two different worlds, and what they witnessed in the garden was a far cry from ordinary Skrying.

"We've had a very exhausting experience, to say the least," Ezekiel says. "Why don't we try to get some rest? We can figure out where we go from here in the morning."

Serenity simply nods as he ushers her to the bedroom. "I'll take the living room. Sleep well," he says, then quickly returns to the other room. He touches a panel. At once the lights lower to a soft, warm glow, and atmospheric music starts to play, lulling them both into a peaceful state of mind. At opposite ends of the dwelling, they feel inexplicably close, yet millions of miles away. Staring out the window into the night sky, Ezekiel wonders what untold fortunes tomorrow will bring. At last he climbs into Lexi's giant leaf hammock and closes his eyes.

Chapter 6

Light and warmth from the late morning sun hits his face. With a stretch, Ezekiel slowly rises from his sleeping place. He's making his way toward the bedroom to check on Serenity when he hears a noise from the kitchen. He peers in to see her sitting in a chair, sipping what he assumes is coffee.

"Good morning."

"Afternoon," she replies with a smile.

Walking over to the counter, Ezekiel waves his hand in front of a machine. "Coffee, black, Costa Rican," he says. The machine instantly starts dispensing the beverage. He turns to look at her. "That doesn't smell like coffee. What is that you're drinking?"

"Iced floral-infused raspberry tea. I don't really care for coffee so late in the morning."

"I take it you slept well, then? Yesterday was crazy, but at least now we're safe."

"Listen, Ezekiel," she says, "there's something I didn't get a chance to tell you the other day. You were honest with me, so I feel it's only right to be honest with you. I'm not who you think I am. I know you know I'm of the privileged class, but in actuality, my father is—"

Before she can finish, the door explodes inward, sending shards of wood flying like spears. He leaps up to shield her from the projectiles. Cons swarm into the room, forming a barrier of lasers and drawn weapons fixed on the two of them.

"Well, isn't this a lovely surprise," Ravana says, parting the wall of Cons to greet the two lovers with a smile. "What a morning, huh? I mean, not only to find Mr. Carthage, who I must say has made the past several days tediously eventful and very stressful, but also to find Mr. Avarice's daughter in his loving arms? It's too fortunate a turn of events, wouldn't you say, Iblis?"

"Indeed. Guess their grace period has run out," Iblis says with a devilish smile that seems to appear out of nowhere.

Shocked, Ezekiel looks over at Serenity. "As in *President* Avarice's daughter?" he asks.

Before she can speak, Ravana bellows, "Move out. Take her home to await her father's arrival. As for Mr. Carthage, President Avarice would like a few words." The Cons move in to apprehend the pair.

"I was trying to tell you before they came in. I'm sorry, Zeke!" Serenity cries out as they're being pulled apart.

"How did you know where to find us?" Ezekiel asks Ravana.

"You shouldn't put your faith in provincial things like friendship. That kind of thinking will always cause pain and trouble," Ravana says before motioning to Iblis to carry Ezekiel away.

Iblis slowly walks over to Ezekiel, smiling. "Time to meet Daddy," he whispers.

꧁꧂

The Cons drag a cuffed Ezekiel into the Oval Office, where an eclectic group of disreputable individuals fixes piercing glares on him. "Well, my colleagues, here he is, the infamous Ezekiel Carthage. Did you know he was even kind enough to look after my daughter? If you will all excuse us, the young lad and I have a lot to talk about."

The rest of the group silently leaves the room, leaving only Avarice, Ezekiel, and several Cons forming a perimeter behind him. "Did you know that Zone Nine headquarters is the former Taj Mahal?" Avarice says. "It was a mausoleum built by the Mughal emperor Shah Jahan in memory of his third wife, Mumtaz Huhal. At the time it was built, people called it the jewel of Muslim artistry. Watchers made it that zone's headquarters and the sector's largest incineration site for processed individuals. The fires there never stop going, day and night. Tragic use of architectural achievement, I must say." He stares off into space, gazing at a map on the wall that shows all the zones and their headquarters.

"Thanks for the history lesson. I'll be sure to note that on the tour guide pamphlet," Ezekiel retorts.

Avarice flashes an evil smile. "I'm glad you still have a sense of humor. You're going to need it. You're fixing to meet my boss, the ambassador to Earth."

A side door opens, revealing Adramelech, who walks over to his pawn while observing Ezekiel. "So this is the trifling creature giving you such a hard time," he says, directing his attention at Avarice. For his part, the president's arrogant stance shrinks until he's cowering and his smugness falls away. "Interesting to see the son picking up where the father left off," Adramelech continues. "I had the privilege of examining him before he was dismembered and eaten."

Ezekiel only stares back at Adramelech, a defiant look on his face.

"That's exactly the way he looked as well. I'm sure you two will have plenty to catch up on in the next life. Ironically, very soon the rest of your species will join you. Once again, your family will be ahead of the curve. Congratulations." With these words, the creature vacates the room, leaving Avarice and Ezekiel alone once again.

"It sure is a malicious thing, isn't it? But it wasn't lying about your father or the rest of our species. They're planning to eliminate the rest of us at the tercentennial. They're going to take all the planet's natural resources before leaving the Earth a barren, dead rock and moving on to the next place." Avarice hangs his head.

"And you're helping them, which makes you even worse than they are," Ezekiel says.

"If I don't, they'll leave me and my family behind to die as well. If I do this, we'll at least be allowed to live under them as slaves and pets. That's why others like me have agreed. Better to preserve what's left of our species while we can."

"Our species doesn't submit to evil and agree to be its servant. To be human means keeping the fire inside the heart alive, even if that means dying with dignity. Tell yourself whatever you want, you self-righteous fool. You're afraid, pure and simple."

Ezekiel's words cause Avarice to lean in closer, staring the young man down. "I suppose just letting us—our history, our species, and way of life—be erased from existence is the better plan? Let me tell you something about humanity: it's survival of the fittest. Adapt or die. I've seen inside the hearts of people, and I know that they crumble when introduced to greed and power. Before that they struggle with the basic emotions of lust, jealousy, hatred, and vengeance. Society is a joke. When it falls away, this race will eat itself alive. I won't allow my daughter to die a miserable death attached to a weak, unimportant human like you. She deserves better, and I will do what I must to see she gets it."

Avarice turns away from Ezekiel. "I hope you enjoyed what time you shared. In twenty-four hours, you'll be entertaining the masses on *Elysian Runner.* I hope you're as enthralling to watch as your father was. Now take him away."

The Cons drag Ezekiel across the floor and out the door to escort him to processing. Outside, the sky begins to cry; a sheet of rain cascades to the earth.

Ezekiel wonders again how they could have been found so quickly. As they approach the exit, he sees Cesare walking in. The two catch each other's eye. The dawning understanding on Ezekiel's face makes Cesare hang his head in shame.

Chapter 7

As the deluge continues to weigh down the planet, Vincent Avarice rides in his luxury vehicle, sighing in relief. Everything is back on track. He pauses in front of his house, wondering what awaits him inside. When he lets himself in, Serenity comes barreling out of the foyer. "Where is he, Father? What did you do with Zeke?"

"So it's Zeke now, is it? Well, I'm sorry to have to inform you, princess, but Zeke will be amusing the crowds during his eradication, compliments of the Running."

"You can't do that! He did nothing wrong!" she cries.

"Sorry, we're all out of options here," he says.

Furious tears run down her face as Serenity comes to see her father for what he truly is. "Another thing. Where's Mother?" she says, her voice filled with anger.

Avarice brushes past her. "Your mother? I'm afraid she left us, my dear. We had a fight the night you disappeared with that trash, and I haven't seen her since. It's just you and me now." He walks into the kitchen, stepping nonchalantly over the coagulated bloodstains that dot the jade marble floor.

Contemplating his current situation, Ezekiel dangles from the ceiling, suspended by chains. He tries to ignore the screams and cries from the other cells and only listen to the voice in his head. He can't make sense of Cesare's actions, nor the fact that Serenity is Vincent Avarice's offspring. But despite his attempts to focus, his thoughts begin to fade away, leaving only one question on his mind: Is she OK?

⚎

"How could you do this, Cesare? Zeke was your friend! Besides, what makes you think they'll keep their end of the deal?" Lexi is enraged, disgusted by his actions.

"They weren't just going to kill him, they were going to come after you and me too. I couldn't bear it if anything happened to you. They assured me that if I cooperated, nothing would happen to either of us, and that we would be set for life. I couldn't keep watching you be degraded and unappreciated. I just wanted to give you everything you could possibly want, all the things I haven't been able to. I did it for you." Cesare's defeated tone says more than his words ever could.

Lexi stares at him, hurt in her eyes. "You're all I ever needed. I'm only happy with you, baby. We're given the hands dealt to us, for whatever reason. It's what we choose to do with this fleeting experience that decides our fate. What matters is in here and here." She points to his heart and head, then kisses him gently and leaves the room, allowing all she's said to sink in.

⚎

The morning sun brings little warmth into his cell. A restless Ezekiel, weary from being chained, hears footsteps approaching and a loud, clanking echo coming closer and closer. The bolt on his cell door slides open. A group of Cons stands in the entrance, the shackle they carry brushing against the cold concrete floor.

Patrons and inquisitive folk alike flock to the stadium in multitudes to catch a glimpse of the man who has caused so much upheaval. Walking down the narrow corridor, Ezekiel sees a light that grows larger and larger along with the commotion outside. A flash of bright light gives way to the sight of the massive stadium, its rows of concrete seating filled by a thousand curious onlookers. All of them roar to life at the sight of the man who's been deemed a terrorist. Led to the center of the arena floor by his metallic wardens, Ezekiel takes a deep breath to calm his nerves.

Standing in the swarm of bloodthirsty enthusiasts and eager watchers, Cesare and Lexi view the spectacle, knowing that their friend is about to be slaughtered for the amusement of others. "Look at him," Lexi says. "He looks so worn down. I don't think I can watch." Cesare remains silent, frozen by the sight of what his betrayal has wrought.

High above the arena floor, Vincent Avarice converses with other members of the Echelon. Serenity sits by his side, silent in her heartbreak. Avarice breaks off his conversation and walks over toward a microphone.

"My fellow citizens, today we are here to pass judgment on one who thinks himself above the law. He has destroyed city propriety and desecrated government facilities put in place to help you, the commoners. He has led many to question not only the intentions of our benevolent caretakers, but also our very way of life. He, along with other agitators, has even brainwashed some of our higher-class citizens with their anarchistic beliefs."

Ezekiel turns to see Cons bringing in a battered, bloody woman. From above, Serenity gasps in horror to see it is Rachael, her mother.

Avarice continues. "These traitors, these vile creatures, worked in league with the barbaric group Origen to plan a systematic assault on the facilities that provide you with clean water and food resources."

The mob roars, throwing stones at the prisoners below and shouting vile obscenities.

"Fortunately," Avarice says, "we have vanquished this threat, and we have at our disposal a swift and just way of dealing with such problematic individuals. Now I submit them to your justice, your judgment, and your enjoyment."

Deafening cheers and applause rise up from commoners and elites alike.

Serenity rushes to Avarice. "Father, what are you doing? Mother hasn't done anything wrong. How could you do this? You must stop at once!" But her pleas fall on deaf ears. He turns away from her, leaving her alone in a box full of wolves in expensive suits.

The Cons unshackle Ezekiel and Rachael before exiting the grounds. Ezekiel stares at the woman beside him for a long time before realizing that her pulpy, trembling face is the same as his lovely Serenity's. Before he can speak, trumpets blare, and the strains of an all-too-familiar song come over the loudspeakers. "Welcome again to another exciting episode of *Elysian Running*!" Malthus says. "Wow, what a great speech from our honorable president to kick off what will surely be a monumental show."

On the far side of the stands of the arena, the force fields lower the titanium gates. Demented screeches echo from the black tunnel. Ezekiel races over to the weapons statue, grabbing a sheathed sword and throwing an automatic bow and a quiver of arrows over his shoulder. He runs to stand in front of Rachael. From the tunnel, six crimson eyes gaze out at the savory meal to come. The clicking of multiple tongues alternates with the loud screeches, and suddenly shadowy figures dash into the light, heading straight for the both of them. Rachael loses all color at the horrifying sight of three Aqrabuamelu. The monstrous creatures have human arms and torsos atop scorpion abdomens.

Ezekiel steadies his bow and takes deadly aim, firing arrows in a frenzy. The creatures disperse, trying to dodge the volley, but an arrow catches one between the eyes, sending it crashing to the ground. The riotous mob shouts its encouragement. Firing his last two arrows, Ezekiel wings another one in the abdomen, slowing it down enough for him to focus on the one leaping into the air, its claws poised to strike.

Unsheathing his sword, Ezekiel slices the creature in half. He spins around, only to catch a glimpse of an Aqrabuamelu pinning Rachael to the ground, piercing her flesh in preparation to devour her. He dives headfirst into the creature, knocking it backward. The Aqrabuamelu and Ezekiel spring up and circle one another, each waiting for the other to make the first move. Letting out an enraged screech, the Aqrabuamelu shoots its pincer from its tail, attempting to ensnare Ezekiel. He rolls out of the way, regaining his footing before slicing the creature's legs off. He jumps on top of the Aqrabuamelu and plunges the blade into its cranium.

The crowd comes alive with passionate applause. Lexi, Cesare, and Serenity smile at Ezekiel's victory. "Did you see that?" Malthus crows. "That has to be the fastest an accused has ever bested sentencing in the first round!"

Avarice's face begins to twitch. He rises from his seat, struggling to regain his composure before he addresses the crowd. "Well done, well done. Do you all see how dangerous these two are? Most would surely have fallen to the Aqrabuamelu, but not them. Their training and brutality, if allowed to be unleashed on our fair city again, would surely have wreaked even more havoc. Proceed with the sentencing."

The crowd cheers him on.

"Father, stop this!" Serenity shouts. "If you ever had a heart or soul, you must have mercy on them!"

"If I were you, I'd sit down," Avarice answers coldly. "It's only because I have a heart that you're not joining them."

Heading to the statue to replenish his ammunition, Ezekiel abruptly stops as howling heralds the Cerberus. The beast comes racing toward him, sidestepping Ezekiel's initial attack. Its sights are set on the weaker prey behind him. It digs its dagger teeth into Rachael, shaking her violently in its jaws and sending pieces of her flying everywhere. Ezekiel can only stand there, stunned. Serenity shrieks in terror at the sight of her mother's gruesome end.

The snarling Cerberus turns to focus on Ezekiel, salivating at the thought of another casualty. Charging ferociously, it throws all of its weight into him, sending Ezekiel flying through the air. He crashes onto his back, disoriented. Recovering, he swiftly avoids being crushed underneath the beast. He plunges his blade into one of the Cerberus's paws. The beast lets out a yelp and flings Ezekiel away, his sword still lodged in the paw. The Cerberus thrusts its elongated fangs at him. Ezekiel grabs it by the jaws, looking down into the maw that would have its meal. The beast begins to run, carrying both of them headlong toward the wall. Ezekiel hastily jumps on its back as the Cerberus collides with the unforgiving cement. Ezekiel promptly lunges for the sword, ripping it from the monster's flesh. Without delay he begins hacking away, severing the Cerberus's head from its body. He collapses next to the bloody remains of claws, fangs, and fur, the roars of the mob filling his ears.

"Marvelous!" Malthus cries. "Indeed, fans, this Ezekiel is proving himself a tough one to put down. I wonder how the Echelon feels about this."

Losing all his composure, Avarice lashes out in fury. "Enough! This has gone on quite long enough!" His colleagues try to calm him, but their words glance off his stony façade. "It's time for this monkey to face a creature known for its undeniable, undefeated streak. We shall see a true battle now. Witness the Behemoth!"

The crowd gasps, then falls deathly silent. The Echelon recoil, cowering far behind Vincent Avarice. The ground begins to quake with the sound of enormous footsteps. A bellow sends shivers through the entire audience, who can hardly stand to watch for the imminent arrival of the petrifying, legendary nightmare.

Standing tall yet exhausted, Ezekiel prepares for what he knows to be the end. Gigantic jagged ivory horns emerge from the shadows, followed by beady yellow eyes attached to a leathery face holding a mouth with legions of teeth almost overtaking the face. The colossal devastator looms over its tiny foe, flicking its reptilian tail and stirring up a cloud of dust. It breathes out, letting off a foul stench followed by a cry that shakes the stadium to its very foundations. Preparing for battle, Ezekiel throws a rebellious look into death's eyes. He's racing toward the monster just as a side of the stadium explodes from the outside, grabbing everyone's attention.

Samson materializes from the haze of debris, adorned in RAMBAM. "Hello, beastie," he says, drawing its attention away from Ezekiel. "That's a lot of ugly." He fires rounds of rocket-propelled grenades into its side, sending it falling, shrieking in pain. Sauntering over to the incapacitated beast, he hammers the suit's foot down on its jaw, lopping off the lower half, then returning the barrel to its face. "Time to be legend once again," he says, and with a single shot, the creature's head explodes everywhere. Finished, Samson sprints to Ezekiel.

"Samson? I thought you were dead."

"Takes more than ET to take me out," Samson says, picking him up as the whole place ignites in a panic. "I pass out only to wake up and find you going gladiator on me? When I said you were a rebel, I didn't think you'd up the ante." Together, the two flee the pandemonium-stricken arena.

"Start the division process, and get Iblis over here with a squadron of Cons. Find them and finish them!" Ravana shouts.

Avarice can only stand there immobile, gawking at the aftermath of the unprecedented escape, numb from the knowledge of the consequences that await him. Out of nowhere, a voice: "You have failed yet once again."

Avarice shakily turns around to face the towering Adramelech. "I did...it was...please..." Avarice tries to force out the words, but Adramelech only snaps his fingers, causing Avarice to explode. His flesh and blood paint the walls of the room. He sighs casually before turning to Ravana and Serenity, the only humans still standing in the room.

"I do hope you are less incompetent than your boss. You will now oversee the continuation of our mutual alliance and acquisitions. Do you think you can serve us more diligently?"

Ravana nods in agreement.

"Ah, Miss Avarice, how lovely to finally meet you in person after hearing so much about you from your father. You know, it's almost unheard of for one such as yourself to exist. Not only a Skry between two classes, but one with such rare beauty as yours. Once in a life-time." Adramelech caresses her hair, sliding his fingers down her face. "Take her. We will use her as bait and lure this perplexing human to us."

Ravana grabs her and rushes out of the room as Iblis appears out of nowhere. "Send out the chiodos, would you?" Adramelech says to Iblis, who silently nods from his place in the shadows.

—※—

"Almost there, amigo, just a little bit farther," Samson says to Ezekiel when they reach the wastes of the outlands on the outskirts of the city.

"Almost where? Where are we going?" Ezekiel says.

"All in good time," Samson replies.

Ezekiel relaxes for a second, looking up into the sky, when he notices blue comets flying in formation. He's never seen such a thing. He grabs Samson's arm, pointing upward. "What's that?" he says, just as the lights start hurtling toward them.

"I don't know, but now's not a time to make a wish," Samson replies, picking up the pace as comets begin crashing around them, flinging earth into the sky.

Samson, not intrigued enough to stop, pushes the RAMBAM suit to its limit as Ezekiel holds on, looking back to see bony hands emerging from the craters. The hands belong to chiodos, large horned creatures the size of the RAMBAM, and their eyes are wreathed in flames.

"Um, must go faster," Ezekiel yells. Crouching into position, the creatures take off after them like bullets. "Do you happen to have any weapons I could use? Or are you planning to speed up?"

"Why, what's the big—" Samson stops as the chiodos appear on either side of them, matching Samson's stride. "Ah!" he cries as two of the creatures move away and start racing back in, preparing to collide with one another, crushing Ezekiel and Samson in the process. Samson launches into the air just in time; the chiodos only hit each other.

"What are those things?" Samson shouts.

"I don't know, but you'd better do something or hand me a weapon!" Ezekiel yells, evading a slash that cuts through the back of the suit, narrowly missing Samson's spine.

Samson turns around and fires rockets into one chiodo's face, sending it flying backward before letting off a small explosion. He protects Ezekiel with his body as they crash and slide on the ground, tumbling head over heels. When they rise again, the two remaining chiodos are closing in.

"I'm low on RPGs, but I've got an idea," Samson says. "All we need to do is make it to that cliff, and we'll be fine."

"What cliff?" Ezekiel says.

"That one." Samson points directly ahead.

Though it's a moonless night, Ezekiel can see they're quickly approaching a massive opening in the ground. "That's not a cliff, that's a canyon! You can't be seriously thinking of jumping that?" he says. Samson only grins and ignites his reserve boosters as he jumps off the edge, catapulting them straight across the opening. He looks over his shoulder to see both creatures following closely behind. "Here, throw this," Samson says, tossing grenades to Ezekiel. The chiodos extend their claws, ready to grab them just as Ezekiel pulls the pins. He hurls the grenades at their pursuers. The explosion sends them both flying into opposite sides of the canyon, where they explode in huge flashes of blue flames.

Ezekiel and Samson finally stop in a patch of tall, dead grass with nothing to keep it company but the trunks of blackened trees and the tune of the wind. Puzzled, Ezekiel is about to ask what's going on when the ground begins to open up, revealing a luminous glow.

"Well," Samson says, "you going in, or you want to take your chances out here?"

Ezekiel hesitantly enters, with Samson right behind him. Together they walk down a dirt path as the ground above them returns to its original place.

Underground, sporadic lines of lighting fill the tunnel. The pathway eventually leads them to an enormous bustling city. Ezekiel can only gaze in astonishment at the vast maze of corridors spiraling deep into the earth.

"I know it's kind of cliché," Samson says. "Underground base of operations where all live and work in a meshed environment. But hey, you know what they say: If it's not broke, why fix it?" He raises an arm toward the city. "Welcome to Origen!"

Chapter 8

"I never knew you were part of Origen. That explains your hospitality. Why didn't you tell me?" Ezekiel asks.

"Didn't know if I could trust you, man," Samson replies. "We've been friends a long time, but you can't ever really know someone 'less you've spilled each other's blood in service for the other, and even then not all is certain."

Ezekiel looks around, absorbing the sights of children playing while their mothers build ammo and armor and men train in hand-to-hand combat. They are shooting or talking stratagem, all covered in dirt, making it nearly impossible to distinguish one from another.

Samson breaks into his reverie. "Most are here because they know the truth of what's really going on. Others are seeking refuge from the craziness since the slums have gotten worse. The rest are here just to fight against the 'ways of true citizenship.'" He chuckles at these last words.

"What truth are you talking about?" Ezekiel says.

Samson stops walking for a moment. "Ezekiel...the Etharchs haven't been here for three hundred years. It's more like a hundred."

Ezekiel's face shows confusion and denial. He's unable to grasp what he's just been told. Samson starts walking again. "Come on. Time you get brought up to speed and meet Origen's leader."

Walls of earth covered in lines of lights give way to digital access strips of ultramodern electrical systems. The men stop in front of two imposing doors, which automatically slide open to reveal an eight-sided room. A man stands in the center. On a slightly raised platform, thirteen other individuals sit around him, all of them shouting. One man's frantic voice rises above the din.

"The Etharchs have moved up their plans by nearly forty-eight hours," he says. "If we don't act now, it'll be too late!"

A woman's voice shoots back, "They'll still want to get all the resources and slave labor off the planet before they risk total annihilation."

The man in the center says calmly, "We all knew that after the events that took place today, they're not going to allow a full-on revolt of the entire planet." His quiet voice somehow cuts through the commotion around him.

"That's Captain Vanaheim," Samson whispers. "He leads the resistance against the Etharchs. Looks like the council is treating him to another belittlement session." He shakes his head. "They're always debating like this. Proves that no matter who you follow, everyone always wants the main chair."

Another council member speaks up. "Until the council decides what to do, we suggest that Vanaheim prepare the initial offense in hopes of a first strike." All the others nod in agreement, except for Vanaheim, whose face betrays his disappointment.

After the council disperses, Samson walks over to Vanaheim. "Seems they're giving you a headache again," he says. "You would think they'd learn how to play well with others."

"Funny," Vanaheim replies, "I was just going to find you to talk about the same thing, along with your escapades in the city today."

"If you ask me, they came into this world complaining, and they're going to leave the same way. They'll just be a little more pompous, that's all."

Vanaheim smiles, but his voice is serious. "Even if they're arrogant, they're still elders. Without them we wouldn't know the truth or have made it this far. Anyway, to business." He looks expectantly at Ezekiel.

"I'm sure my friend here needs no introduction," Samson says.

Vanaheim nods, clasping Ezekiel's hand. "It's a privilege to meet you, Ezekiel. Haven't seen a display of defiance like that since your father's. He was a good man."

"You knew my father?" Ezekiel says.

"Your mother too. They were both members, which means this is in your blood. Your father and I were two men cut from the same cloth, you might say. Bravest man I knew, and hell of a drinker to boot." Vanaheim's eyes cloud over. "Near the end, shortly after your mother was executed, your father started growing detached. He became increasingly caught up in the flames of retribution. Nothing else mattered to him, including taking care of you, the person he loved most. He couldn't think of anything but vengeance."

Samson breaks in. "Zeke here was wondering what the truth of the Etharchs was."

Vanaheim nods. "Follow me. I'll give you the answers you seek."

He leads Ezekiel to his private quarters. The walls of the small office are adorned with ancient books. "So you want truth, do you?" He pours a glass of wine, inhaling its scent with a deep sigh. "Well, my friend, they say the truth is always unbearable and unbelievable, yet echoes in the bones with a resilience that lies don't possess. What you have perceived as centuries of control and enslavement in actuality is little more than a century. We don't know how they did it, but it seems that humanity has had its history, our very minds, whitewashed." He begins pacing around the room. "In the middle of the twenty-first century, our ancestors encountered a signal from space. On trying to communicate with it, they found a voice on the other end. This voice told them that there was something more to our existence than we could perceive with the naked eye. They told us that they were a peaceful yet strict people who had been warring since time was time with another species, whose very nature was evil, an evil that was bent on devouring everything in its path.

"The government heads and leaders of our world held a historic intergalactic meeting with the extraterrestrials, who soon became known as Etharchs. Our leaders decided to make a pact with them. In exchange for their knowledge, we would allow them to reside on this planet, to regroup and figure a way to rebuild their forces, hidden from their enemies." He sighed. "Unfortunately, the Etharchs lied. They were the warlike species, filled with hungry anger and a lust for domination and all things unholy. By the time our leaders realized their mistake, it was already too late. To prevent our extinction, an agreement was signed. We would become slaves to them on our world. As the true nature of the agreement started to emerge, a few individuals found out the truth. They tried to spread the news about what they had found out, to warn people. In response, the Etharchs formed an order called the Convergence on Negation, or Cons. The men in this order worked hand in hand with the Etharchs to prevent the truth from coming out by any means necessary. But though they were effective, even they couldn't hide the truth entirely.

"Well, as you can imagine, when the good people of Earth eventually found out about the pact, they fought back bravely. Yet it was futile. The fighting left most of the world barren. The Etharchs used the survivors to not only maintain the remnants of our race, but to do their bidding. This is how the Skry came to be. The biological imprint is designed to control our reproductive capabilities, causing most to never marry nor bear offspring. It maintains the population while also making us easy to control. Slowly but surely, two social classes emerged, upper and lower. On the one side were the entitled, privileged few who were allowed to live comfortably so long as they kept the rest in line, even if that meant the eradication of others. On the other side were the poor and meek, who struggled merely to survive. These people became more compliant due to dwindling resources and numbers and soon became the world's labor force, slaves to the will of the Echelon and Etharchs. Your father, after your mother died, couldn't bear the thought of you growing up in a world rigged to lose, so he attempted a coup. You know what the sad result of that was."

Vanaheim pours another glass, again inhaling it deeply. He releases a sigh through his teeth. "However, irony resides in all things. The key to undoing our enslavement lies in our enslavement itself. If two people from the opposing classes joined in union, it would negate the Skrying, overriding the system and causing it to crash. Hence the barriers and Cons to keep us in line and to prevent the classes from ever mingling."

Silence fills the room. Ezekiel is the first to break it. "I have Skried to Vincent Avarice's daughter, Serenity."

Samson and Vanaheim glance at each other incredulously. "Can this be so?" Vanaheim says. "Could one in our midst actually have Skried to an elite?"

"It's true," Ezekiel says. "Samson, I was bringing her to see you the night I left, but when I came back and saw your barge was on fire, I thought you were dead." He turns to Vanaheim. "Look, by now they have her. We need to rescue her. She's not like the rest of them; she's good, purehearted. I never thought I would meet someone like her."

Vanaheim and Samson are silent for a long moment. Finally Vanaheim says, "All right. If you say she's not like them, then she isn't. Furthermore, you two could end this tyrannical regime that plagues all of us. The only problem is convincing the council. They feel it is best to launch a full-scale attack on each of the zone headquarters simultaneously. They plan to infiltrate the buildings with missiles from the past as a final insult to the Etharchs. The problem is, the missiles themselves would destroy not only their headquarters, but the cities and surrounding lands. I personally believe it's asinine to use weapons of mass destruction. Past generations wouldn't use the missiles unless left with no choice; even the Etharchs have avoided using them. We may finish off what's left of the planet if we do."

"So let's convince them not to—persuade them to do things our way, the right way," Ezekiel says. The three look at each other, nodding in agreement.

"Hell," Samson says enthusiastically, "looks like I get to join you this time in a little destructive rebellion. Maybe if I'm lucky, I'll piss off some wise sages in the process."

⚌⚍

Riots ravage the streets as fires engulf a city already on the edge. Cons detain anyone unlucky enough to be caught, and gun down those who won't comply. Far out of reach of the chaos, in a luxury prison, Serenity impatiently awaits her fate, her thoughts on the day's events. Her parents are dead, one by the other's decree and one obliterated in the blink of an eye for his failures. But none of this occupies her mind as much as Ezekiel.

Ravana walks in to check on his prisoner. "I see the festivities outside aren't dampening your spirits any further."

"When can I leave here?" she asks.

"All in due time, lovely. You're a valuable commodity, a means to an end, so to speak. Our benevolent caretakers feel you could be just the one to bring both your lover and the rest of the resistance out of hiding. We'll be able to crush them all in one swift stroke."

"How can you work for them? They'll kill you without a second thought, just like they're killing those people on the streets."

"True, the thought has crossed my mind," he says. "But needless to say, steps have been taken to ensure my longevity among the living. Better to be at the right hand of the devil than in his way, wouldn't you agree?"

"No. I would rather die with dignity than crawling on all fours like a beast," she says, her eyes flashing with anger.

"Truly, you're more like your mother in spirit and vigor than your old man. That's why he broke said spirit before you were born. He told the Etharchs to inject her nervous system with a highly addictive substance. It made her docile and compliant. Until the end, that is." He smiled. "It's funny how far they both went, trying to try to control their environment and everyone around them, only to have it blow up in their faces."

Serenity is flooded with mixed emotions. "If this is to be my prison, I would rather be alone than have you as company." She spits at him.

"Very well. Yet one does need to socialize. So I bring you a present, some companionship." He waves his hand, and Lexi is thrown into the room. "You see? We, the masters and I, can have moments of generosity, even if it's the unbearable company of a half-breed." He looks down at Lexi with disdain. "Enjoy." The door slams shut behind him.

Serenity runs over to help Lexi up. "Are you OK? It seems you too are a prisoner here."

"Yes," Lexi says sadly. "They want Cesare, but he vanished when everything went awry today. They're holding me in the hope of acquiring him for more information." She gives a small, hard laugh. "They don't seem to know that no one wants to be seen with a half-breed." She looks at Serenity. "How are you holding up? I'm sorry about your mother. That was a terrible way to go."

Serenity looks down at the floor. "At least she's at peace now, not suffering this world anymore. I'm just so worried about Ezekiel. No one knows where he is, or if he's even alive."

"Don't worry about Zeke," she says. "If I know him, he's quite all right and will do whatever it takes to save you, whether it's with his life or death."

Serenity sighs. "That's what worries me."

※

Back at Origen headquarters, Ezekiel convenes the council to explain his predicament, along with the plans that would allow an alternative to the missiles. After he's finished, one of the elders speaks. "We have heard your plan, and although it seems plausible and less destructive, there is too much at stake to try to risk it for the sake of love and hope. I'm sorry, my son. We have decided."

A brief moment of hopelessness enters Ezekiel's mind. In desperation he blurts out, "The tercentennial is in one week. Give us that long to slow down their operations and allow us the chance at an alternative."

The elders ponder his request. "And how would you slow down their operations?" the head elder asks him.

"By taking out the facilities that are robbing the planet of natural resources, hitting both groups where it hurts the most."

They all talk among themselves, intrigued by the proposal. "Very well, you have until the eve of the tercentennial to hinder their progress. If you can't, we will continue as planned." The council disperses, leaving Ezekiel, Samson, and Vanaheim alone.

"Nice job," Samson says. "So where do you want to start?"

"We start with Liquidation. With Avarice gone, that will be the easiest target," Ezekiel says with determination.

⸻

"Wretches and kings, we're coming for you," Ezekiel says with a grin as he prepares for the mission. The look on Samson's faces causes him to stop.

"What?" Ezekiel says.

"Nothing. I just think it's funny how all this time you could have been part of the club. We could have been doing this together ages ago," Samson says.

"Nah, everything has its place under the sun. This couldn't have happened any other way."

"How you handled the council and seeing how receptive they were to you, your plan to take on each facility that's stealing our resources…you may not want to see it, but you were made for this."

"He's right, you know," Vanaheim says, looking Ezekiel over. "Seeing you there dressed the way you are, you're the image of your father, with one difference: you are fighting for righteousness and love, not a vendetta or hatred." He puts his hand on Ezekiel's shoulder. "We move out in thirty. Meet me on the platform." He leaves to prepare his men.

Vanaheim looks over the squadron of men ready for whatever lies ahead. Glancing at each of them one by one, he nods in approval before debriefing them. "Men, you are here because like the rest of Origen, you believe in a cause, a cause bigger than personal motivations or desires, a cause that will decide the fate of humanity. Today we have a chance to cure this planet of the disease from space and free all of us from total devastation. We are heading up to Liquidation, the main facility where the Echelon and Etharchs control the fresh water in Zone One. This is a time-sensitive mission and must succeed no matter the cost. If it does not, it will leave the elders with no other option but to detonate a bomb so devastating, there will be nothing left to fight for. Ask yourselves this question: If you can end the fascists' regimes and save countless lives, isn't that worth dying for?" He scans the men in front of him, all of whom are listening attentively. "Gentlemen," he says, "good luck and Godspeed."

⚔

Samson turns to Ezekiel. "You ready for some fun?" he says.

Airborne and racing off to the facility, Ezekiel can still think of nothing but Serenity. The deep wound of not having her in his arms leaves him wanting. Trying to shake it off, he goes through the plan again in his mind before Samson plops down beside him.

"So, what's the big plan?" Samson says.

"Figured we could sneak in, taking out anyone in our way, set up explosives, and flee before it all blows up."

A look of shock passes over Samson's face. But all he says is, "Sounds good." He rises to his feet. "All right, ladies, mount up. We're fixing to rain down on this facility like fire and brimstone." The rest of the team stands up, all waiting for the go signal. The lights go out and the hull turns red as the hangar bay opens to the night sky. Ezekiel closes his eyes and takes a deep breath as one by one they all jump out of the plane. Hurling toward the earth, he looks out at the spectacular sight of lakes holding the largest remaining supply of fresh water, smack in the middle of Zone One.

Landing quietly on Liquidation premises, the squadron covertly makes its way to the pipeline. Ezekiel says, "All right, men, here's where we break into teams. Team One will go with Samson and rig the pipes and facilities with the bombs. Team Two will come with me to shut down the system and set up the detonation devices."

They break off and go their separate ways. Samson and Ezekiel look at one another, silently wishing each other good luck before joining their teams.

Samson and his team quietly take care of the guards who stand watch, looking for suspicious activity or movement. Setting up the explosives and charging them up, he looks over to confirm with his squad that they are good to go.

"Five by five, Zeke. We're all set here," he says.

"Copy that. Making our approach now," Ezekiel replies as his crew makes its way up to the giant building, heading toward the main servers. Creeping around a corner, he narrowly misses being shot by a guard. "Welcome to the Great Lakes, Ezekiel!" a voice cries out, followed by an endless barrage of bullets. Ezekiel and his team return fire as both sides start losing men quickly.

"Hold your fire!" the voice calls out to his guards. Silence descends before the voice speaks again. "We haven't been properly introduced. My name is Thetan Haram. I have to thank you for your brilliant display of defiance the other day. Because of that, Avarice is dead, and I am now in charge of Liquidation. Now that he is gone, we all have comfortable positions of power. However, as much as I and the others would like to thank you, I'm afraid this is where your road ends." Thetan gives the signal to his troops to recommence shooting in Ezekiel's direction.

Pinned down and with no exit in sight, Ezekiel grows frustrated. He's about to charge to his own death when an explosion coming from Thetan's direction goes off, causing everyone to take cover. Ezekiel looks over to see Samson hanging off the building, a grenade launcher in his hand.

"Couldn't find the doorbell, so I decided to just come in," Samson shouts, firing another round that sends Thetan and his men scattering in opposite directions. Jumping down, he walks over to Ezekiel and gives him a hand up. "How many times am I going to have to save you? Really, I should start charging a service fee." He laughs, unaware that Thetan is standing behind him and taking aim. Ezekiel pushes Samson out of the way. The shot meant for Samson hits him, but it doesn't stop him from charging headlong into Thetan and pushing him out the window. The two men look out as he squeals, plummeting to his death.

Samson examines Ezekiel's wound, seeing if it went in and out. "You sure have something or someone watching over you," he says. He helps him make his way across the floor and out of the building. Together they run to the rendezvous point and call for their ride. As the plane hovers several feet above the ground, they hastily make their getaway just before detonating the bombs, sending the entire facility bursting into the sky in a brilliant display of fire.

"Where to next, oh fearless leader?" Samson says.

"I think it's time to get some fresh air," Ezekiel answers, smiling as they blast through the night sky and make their way toward Zone Three. "Hey, did you put that call in to Vanaheim?"

"Of course," Samson says. "He thought it was a great idea to touch base with our associates over in the east. He even gave word to an old war buddy of his who's expected to meet us when we land. How long do you think before news hits the elite?"

"Don't know," Ezekiel says. "But once it does, they'll be squirming in their seats." They both begin to laugh.

Ravana starts slamming furniture across his office when word reaches him that Liquidation is no more. A hologram of Adramelech appears, halting his violent mood swing.

"I thought I made myself clear. You were supposed to preside over your new office diligently," Adramelech says with vehemence.

"I will handle it, sir. Let's just see how well he does when I put his little girlfriend on display to the world!" Ravana says.

A look of grudging approval comes over Adramelech's face. "Then see it done," he says before dissipating.

The morning sun rises elegantly with the promise of a brighter day than ever before as Ezekiel looks out at the ancient and mysterious islands in Zone Three. The plane finally sets down and rolls to a stop. When Samson and Ezekiel emerge, an older Japanese man stands waiting patiently, his back ramrod straight. "Gentlemen, welcome to Zone Three. I am Admiral Hasegawa, and I am good friends with Vanaheim." They both walk up and salute him.

"Vanaheim told me to watch out for the one who is called Samson," he says. "I was told to lock up all liquor."

Samson's face turns sour, as if he just ate something really bad. Hasegawa turns to Ezekiel. "Then that must mean you are Zeke. It is an honor to meet you. I have been keeping up with all your recent escapades." Ezekiel nods humbly.

Immediately heading toward central command, Hasegawa updates them on their best line of attack on the Siphon facility. "This will not be as easy as the last one you did. Unlike the other industrial units, this one floats several miles above the earth's surface, out in the middle of the Pacific Ocean. That's the surest way for it to extract oxygen before it starts meddling with other elements. The steel fortress is suspended by four gigantic generators that shoot electrical rays downward, producing the force needed to keep it afloat. We need to disable the shields first before we can shoot missiles at the generators. In addition, it is covered by a flying armada of drone Cons, all equipped to bring down planes bigger than seven-fifty-sevens."

"I thought you said it was going to be difficult," Samson says as he pulls a flask out of his armor. Ezekiel and Hasegawa look at each other before staring Samson down. "What?" he says. "I knew Vanaheim—the old salt *would* give you a heads up on my recreational activities." Samson smiles as Ezekiel just shakes his head.

"OK," Ezekiel says, "so what we need from you, Admiral, are some of your finest pilots loaded up with enough ammo and missiles to buy us the time we need to disable the shields and put the floating plant down for good. Can you help us with that?"

Hasegawa simply smiles and nods in agreement. "Good," Ezekiel says. "We leave now."

⚏

Ravana storms into Serenity's cell, catching her and Lexi by surprise. Without any words, he walks up and proceeds to drag her forcefully to the door.

"What are you doing? Let her go!" Lexi cries, trying to stop him. He knocks her to the floor, then grabs a handful of her hair, pulling her up until they're face to face.

"Your boyfriend has officially overstayed his welcome with the council. Now it's your turn to prove your usefulness by bringing him out of hiding."

"I'll never help you!" she says defiantly as he continues to jerk her around.

"Oh, you will help," he says, "whether you want to or not."

⚎

Engines fueled with purpose spur the fleet of resistance fighters headlong toward Siphon. "There it is," Samson says to Ezekiel, staring at the mechanized goliath as it pulls in fresh air from the stratosphere. Deafening magnetic generators suspend it miles above the earth's surface. Just then the factory's aerial task force comes into view, bearing down on them. Ezekiel radios the resistance fighter jets: "Divert all enemy aircrafts. We need enough time to get close enough to attach and land on it." At his words, the jets blast forward, engaging the enemy pilots in a furious exchange of bullets. Jets explode in the air as Samson and Ezekiel's plane maneuvers through the chaos, edging closer as they head to the hangar bay to prepare.

"You ready for this?" Samson says to Ezekiel.

Ezekiel gives him a look. "Let's find out."

As the bay door opens, a torrent of wind beats down on them. They take a second to calculate their trajectory before leaping out into the cold air as debris from the conflict rains down around them. Freefalling with incredible speed, they crash hard on the plant's smooth outer surface, nearly tumbling to the edge and sliding right off the factory. But before they can fall, Samson takes out his dagger, slams it into the side of the building, and grabs Ezekiel by the hand, causing them both to crash through a glass skylight. Shooting off a steel cable, they just miss colliding with the merciless floor.

"That was intense," Samson says, chuckling under his breath as he unhooks them both from their parachutes. Once they're free, they begin to climb down to the control room.

"So where do you think the main hub is?" Samson says.

"Usually in a place like this it would be near the shield generator, to keep everything close by case of an emergency," Ezekiel says. Rapidly descending the building's metal skeleton structure, Ezekiel suddenly starts to get a bad feeling as they approach the massive control system. "It shouldn't be this easy," he says.

"I know. No form of confrontation whatsoever," Samson replies.

Suddenly a screen drops and a man appears. "I am Mokushiroku. So good to see you made it this far," he says. "Unfortunately, it was for nothing. We have set small tactical explosives guaranteed to take out anyone who tries to disable the system, without harming the plant itself. In other words, you have been defeated, and this is where your tale ends. I'm truly sorry you came all this way for nothing." He laughs before the transmission cuts out.

"Well, that sucks," Samson says. "We came all this way for nothing."

"No, we didn't," Ezekiel says as he begins pulling up schematics of the place at the nearby main computer. He points. "There. All we have to do is fly a plane straight into the extraction system itself. We do that, this whole place will blow."

"Well, that's great, but how do you plan on doing that?"

"By commandeering one of the planes."

"What? You're crazy!" Samson says.

"Look, this metal thief must go down regardless of whether we live or die. The facility's jets are nothing more than oversized drones. I'll just hack into the system and reprogram one to carry me in to make sure it all goes to plan," Ezekiel says.

"Why don't we just navigate it?"

"Because the magnetic system will disrupt any automatic aircraft. That's why they themselves have mini disruptors, so they won't short-circuit."

"Then it should be me. I've always wanted to go out with my boots on, and you're too important to the resistance."

"I can't ask you to do that, Samson. I wouldn't ask anyone to take my place in doing something I personally know would kill them. Besides, you're a valuable asset too."

While the two men argue over who will be sacrificed, overhead a resistance fighter and a drone collide, causing both to fall into the system itself. The place begins to implode.

"What's going on?" Samson yells.

"Apparently two planes took our idea," Ezekiel says.

"Well, guess that solves that dilemma. Now let's get out of here!" Samson says as they race for the safest exit.

Lungs begin to trade oxygen for battery acid as the two flee from the unstable plant crumbling before their very feet. Faster and faster, they try to make it across a skyline underneath a line of exploding generators. Without warning, the whole bottom of Siphon gives way, ejecting them into open air miles above the ocean. They both fall headfirst. Ezekiel looks over at his comrade, and his mind shifts to Serenity, accepting the fact that he will never see her again and tell her how much she means to him.

Suddenly, ripping through the chaos and clouds, a helicopter scoops them up, banging them against metal and seats. Samson laughs. "Who says miracles don't exist?" Both men look up to see Admiral Hasegawa at the helm of the chopper. Siphon plummets out of the air as they whoop and holler, watching the floating menace nosedive into the ocean. Before it sinks beneath the waves, it explodes one more time, any evidence it ever existed totally obliterated.

Landing back at Origen headquarters, the celebration is cut short as several guards wait for them to descend out of the plane. "You should be happy," Samson says with a smile. "Water and air are officially free now."

Vanaheim levels a serious stare at Samson and then switches his glance to Ezekiel.

"What is it?" Ezekiel says. "What's wrong?"

A guard tells them to come with him. Concerned and unsure of what is going on, they follow the guard into the communications room, where he pulls up the feed Ravana has just put out. Ezekiel looks on in horror as Ravana holds Serenity forcefully in front of the camera.

"Citizens of Zone One," he says, "this girl standing before you is the daughter of the late Vincent Avarice. She is also the Skried lover of the terrorist Ezekiel Carthage. This enemy of peace and prosperity has destroyed the way we harness air and water, furthering his ambitions of bringing pain and suffering to us all. Tomorrow I shall execute here, live, Avarice's daughter in the Purification Purge, as a lesson to both classes that there is a new zero-tolerance policy. This message goes out to Mr. Carthage: if you want to keep her from this fate, you will turn yourself over immediately for termination. You have until dawn."

The feed cuts out as Samson and Vanaheim both look at Ezekiel. He screams in a murderous rage before the two subdue him long enough to talk some sense into him.

"Let go of me!" he tells them.

"I know what she means to you, I do, but we can't afford to lose you," Vanaheim says.

"She's all that matters. I don't care if I die tomorrow. At any rate, if either of us dies, then our original plan fails, and Origen drops the bombs anyway. So why can't I just end this?"

"Because unlike her, you have become a symbol of rebellion. Because of you, countless individuals are now rising up against the Etharchs and their grunts. If you Skried to an elite, there are plenty of chances we'll find another pair, right, Vanaheim?" Samson says.

"No, not really," Vanaheim answers. "The odds of this happening again are impossible. The truth is that we need you, and if you go down this path, you will be following in your father's footsteps and giving yourself over for nothing but vengeance when there is a bigger picture to consider."

At his words, Ezekiel starts calming down and they release him. He ponders what they said for several seconds before answering. "My father died because he finally had enough of being told who lives and who dies. Of evil entities with only selfish reasoning getting to decide who is entitled to have it all while the rest wallow in misery and suffering. I understand his actions now. When they take away your hope, faith, and life, there's nothing but darkness. She is my light, and I will not see it snuffed out. So if that means letting them win their pathetic display of who's in charge, then so be it." With that he walks away from them. They both look at each other. Without a word, Vanaheim coldcocks Ezekiel from behind, forcing him to the ground hard.

Surging images of Serenity and all who mattered in his life flash by before he is transported to a plain of endlessness. Sky and land go on forever, and hundreds of puddles are dispersed here and there. Gazing around, his attention is drawn to four colossal stone pillars standing in a straight line. Apprehensive, he makes way over to them.

"Ezekiel Carthage. We have been expecting you."

Chapter 9

"Where am I?" he says to the extremely large sandstone columns.

"You are in the Boundless Terra Firma. A place that has no beginning or end, just consistency ruled over by us."

"Who are you?" he says.

"We are the Zeitgeist," says one. "Pillars of time. We represent the fabric of epochs in space and dimensions. Spirits who give assistance in every period of every age in the struggles against evil, we are Past, Present, Future, and Eternal. We hold the records of every generation, period, and era in the entire universe." It is the pillar called Present.

"OK, so how did I get here then?" he asks.

"You are here because of that which affects all—the unraveling of everything. You were transported here to bear witness and deliver a message," Past says. Ezekiel stands silent, humbled and vexed at what he's hearing as he waits for his next unasked question to be answered.

The pillar called Future speaks. "You are one of very few graced with a glimpse of all that is, and with a privileged audience with us. All that you have done since your meeting with the one Skried to you, the one known as Serenity, has heralded actions destined to bring about foretold events. What will soon come to pass has begun to cause ripples throughout the cosmos that will affect every living soul and thing. Most are not prepared for this, nor could they ever be."

"I don't understand. You're saying the bond between Serenity and I will alter the course of time and space?"

"No, that which is will always be. You have only allowed dramatic events to unfold at the appropriated time." In unison, the Pillars say, "What will be, will be."

"So what happens now?" he asks.

"You wake up," Eternity says. "But be forewarned: time is not on your side. Each person has a part to play, be it significant or otherwise. All are necessary."

In a flash Ezekiel awakens in a darkened room, dazed and in pain, holding his head where he was hit. The sudden realization of what happened causes him to jump up quickly. He tries to open the door, only to find it locked. Ezekiel starts wailing and banging on the door, demanding to be released, before Samson appears and opens it.

"What time is it?" Ezekiel barks at him.

"It's noon, the day before the tercentennial," Samson says.

Ezekiel's eyes grow large. Serenity is already gone, then. He lunges in anger at Samson and punches him before guards pull him off.

"She's not dead, Zeke!" Samson says.

"How? How is that possible? I was supposed to turn myself in at dawn or they would incinerate her."

"You did," Samson says.

Ezekiel stares at him, confusion etched into his face. Without another word, Samson leads his friend down the steel corridor back into the communications room. There the elders of Origen and Vanaheim are waiting for him.

"Good to see you up and calm, my son," one of the elders says to him. "Sorry for keeping you out for so long. We had much to discuss and knew the importance of her safety would cause a lot to hang in the balance."

"What's going on? How is it she is still alive if I'm with you?" he says to them.

Vanaheim pulls up a feed. Ezekiel looks on in disbelief at the screen as he watches what appears to be footage of him giving up and being subsequently executed in the Running. He turns back to the elders. "I don't understand," he says.

"We had a decoy take your place," Vanaheim says.

"A decoy?"

"Yes," the head elder says. "We took a willing volunteer to have facial reconstruction to make him look like you. At dawn he turned himself in, saving Serenity from further harm." A live feed of Serenity, safely back in the high-rise prison, flashes onto the screen.

"You're telling me you had a man take my place and sacrifice himself?" Ezekiel says.

"No, we had a volunteer take your place and give his life for you and the cause," Vanaheim says. "This is why we couldn't let you do it. You've already inspired so many. There's no telling where this will go."

The head elder adds, "Unfortunately, though you made a noble attempt to save lives and avert the bombings, plans to bomb each zone will start tomorrow as planned."

"But why?" Ezekiel asks. "We were making great progress. We destroyed Liquidation. Who's to say the rest won't fall like that facility?"

"Because after it fell, Ravana had the others triple their security forces, and because time is of the essence, we cannot wait any longer for your plan to play out. I'm sorry," the elder says.

"So what happens to the people of Zone One, and to Serenity?"

"She and others will die for the noble cause of the liberation and continuation of humanity."

"So you're all telling me that my life is more valuable than hers? Who are you to decide which life is precious or worthless? That's exactly the mindset we're trying to overthrow!" But his words fall on deaf ears. The elders depart, leaving him, Samson, and Vanaheim alone.

"Crazy old cooks. They'd rather see the world in ashes than listen to reason," Samson says in irritation.

"I believe there is a way to beat them to the punch," Vanaheim says. "And if it doesn't work, they can still go ahead with their plan. C'est la vie. Come with me." He hurries both men to the launch pad. "It's risky and has the potential to be a suicide mission, but it just might work. All we need is someone crazy enough to pilot through the abandoned underground railway system." Vanaheim and Ezekiel both look at Samson.

"Like you have to ask," Samson says with a smile.

Taking care not to attract attention, they quickly sneak to the runway. When they reach it, they gaze at one of the last small stealth drone fighters ever made. Vanaheim says, "This lovely antique is the X-47 B Drone, king of the skies in its day. This little baby has been gutted and revamped with up-to-date technology. It'll get you two wherever you need to go. Not only that, it's fast, and the wingspan is short enough to make it through the tunnels without crashing into the walls." He turns to the two men. "I'll stall for you two as long as possible. But if they fire the missiles, you'll only have about five minutes before they land, and then it's game over."

"Five minutes? Why don't you make it a challenge for us?" Samson says.

"Also, the way may be flooded with downed electrical wires, so try not to divulge Samson's lack of driving capabilities as much as possible. Good luck, Ezekiel. I hope you find her and come back alive. I'd like to tell you more about your father and buy you a drink someday when this is all over." He gives them the OK to go as security tries to tell them to shut down the ship.

"Well, amigo, this should be fun," Samson says. "If we succeed, just remember one thing: chicks dig scars." He ignites the jet engines, blasting them into the air.

As they barrel down the decrepit underground system, pieces of the cavern fall from directly above them. Samson dives, avoiding collision at breakneck speeds.

"Oh, man, I'm glad I didn't eat," Ezekiel says.

"Relax, this is a breeze, man," Samson says, dodging more debris. He doesn't notice the hidden security measurements nearby. A sudden explosion forces the jet slightly into the wall. They look back to see a ball of fire rushing down the tunnel toward them. The tunnel itself is caving in.

"Least this makes it more interesting," Samson says through clenched teeth.

"Don't you have some kind of cliché about this to alleviate our dire circumstances?" Ezekiel asks.

"Nope. Figured I would just fly and try not to kill us."

"Oh...OK, you do that," Ezekiel says. The walls quickly start to close in around them as metal and concrete touch, making sparks hit the oil spatters and downed wires that litter the ground. Another explosion erupts a few feet behind them, sending the jet's tail into the roof and shutting down the right engine.

"Well...that's not good," Samson says. "This trip may be over before it starts." Nevertheless, he keeps pushing the limit of the aircraft as best he can. There's a veer-off directly ahead, but the impending doom behind them lurches closer and closer.

Making a final attempt to recover, Samson inverts the jet, sending it to the left and out of harm's way. "This is a fun ride, isn't it?" Samson yells over the noise. Ezekiel just sighs with relief.

They're almost at the end of the tunnel when another hidden security device goes off, blowing up the back end of the jet. They spiral into the walls, the jet spinning violently until it crashes at their destination. They activate the escape hatch, popping the canopy roof and hurtling beside the destroyed craft as dust fills the air.

"Another happy landing," Ezekiel says, sighing.

"Thank you for choosing us for your flight needs," Samson says. "Please exit the dilapidated aircraft in an orderly fashion, and I hope you enjoy the rest of your day, which may be your last."

Hiking through the rubble, the two climb over boulders and twisted metal. Eventually they reach a tall flight of stairs. Trekking up and up, they finally reach the end of one leg of their journey on the way to the mission.

"So what's next?" Samson asks.

"We head a few yards east of here. We'll exit near the entrance to zone headquarters," Ezekiel says.

"You sure?" Samson says, his breath ragged from climbing. "I mean, don't get me wrong, I believe you're Skried to her and all, but how do you know she's even up there? It's not like that thing's got compass that says, 'Hey, make a left in five-point-three yards.'"

"I just know. Call it faith, man," Ezekiel says, looking back at his friend as they pick up the pace. Making their way to a door, they gather their courage before opening it. When they do, they find the street outside littered with bodies. All around, in stacks up to their torsos, are the men, women, and children who once walked these very streets. A mixture of emotions fills the two.

"I guess it's beginning. These people, they...I can't even see the road," Samson says in shock.

Ezekiel's voice is grim. "We've got to get moving. No time to waste."

Suddenly the dead silence gives way to incongruous cheering nearby. From where they are, Ezekiel and Samson can just make out the hordes of civilians gathering on streets decorated for the festivities. An assortment of flags and streamers surrounds Zone One headquarters, along with a joyous crowd, as Malthus takes center stage.

"What a wonderful turnout we have here today to celebrate our tercentennial!" he says. "Over the past several weeks, we have all been forced to deal with terrible tragedy and horrifying ordeals. Terrorists have laid siege to our city, stolen peace from our very bosoms, and just recently, we found out that our great and wonderful president was killed in that horrible attack on our justice system, which enforces our security, prosperity, and entertainment. At the request of our fair system and the benevolent caretakers, we would like to take a moment of silence for the man who strived not just to unify this zone and our city, but also to protect the very way we live."

Ezekiel and Samson find discarded clothes in a nearby alley. They take the ragged shrouds and disguise themselves before making their way through the zealots watching a montage dedicated to Vincent Avarice. The ghastly display of false information and phony martyrdom makes Ezekiel gag, but he's able to make his way steadily through the crowd, which seems to fill every empty space possible. He stops; from the corner of his eye, he can see Serenity and Lexi in front of the audience. It makes his heart skip a beat, and his forearm begins pulsating. The ladies have been made to dress in respectable attire, paraded out to show cooperation and allegiance to the powers that be.

"I have never worn such a lovely outfit before," Lexi says to Serenity. "Of course, it doesn't make up for the atrocities to the ears and eyes. Sorry you're being displayed like this."

Serenity says nothing. She looks drained of life and even her very will to live, until she feels her arm beginning to pulsate. She inconspicuously gazes down at her Skry, which is glowing with rapid precision, signaling that Zeke is nearby. She can't believe it: she saw his brutal execution with her own eyes and has been bleeding the tears of a broken heart ever since. Now life invigorates her face. Lexi glances at her, sensing something is up.

The dedication montage ends with thunderous cheers, and Malthus retakes center stage. "Now, my friends, it is time for the celebration of the three hundredth anniversary of our rescue from extinction by our liberators, the Etharchs! Presenting our ambassador to Earth and humanity. You know him by his great deeds and endless devotion to you all. It is my considerable pleasure to introduce… Adramelech!"

The applause is overwhelming, and trumpets blare in the background. Adramelech comes forward to address the crowd.

"When we arrived on this world, it was near desolation. The overwhelming strife caused by the trifling debacles that plague many planets, including yours, had reduced Earth to a decaying state. Greed, religious persecution, sexism, ignorance—all devastated your civilization and nearly destroyed life as we know it. However, we saw something here on Earth and in its inhabitants that we hadn't witnessed in countless other galaxies: the true potential in each and every living soul to make unprecedented change and turn the tide. The collective gathering known to you as the Etharchs has existed far longer than one of your millennia, and we have found the true way to coexist peacefully, not just among ourselves, but with other races and species as well. We have worked to share this great knowledge with you for three centuries now." Adramelech's voice entrances all who give him their ears. He continues: "Now the time is here once again to quell the rising tide of terrorism and radicalism, which selfishly serves the individual, with no care or consideration for the collective population. We must fight to keep hope alive and bring peace to countless generations to come. Today we stand at the threshold of a new dawn, one that holds no further mourning. Let the festivities start!" The multitude of brainwashed citizens shakes the very ground with their enthusiastic yells.

"We haven't much time," Samson whispers to Ezekiel. "The council will soon be sending those nice party favors here to crash the festivities."

Ezekiel nods in agreement. They both inch closer and closer to the stage, weaving through the cheering throng. From the front of the audience, Serenity frantically searches for Ezekiel while giving no sign that she knows he is nearby. She spots him only feet away at the same time as he notices her. They gaze at each other, allowing the world to fall away from that moment, halting time itself. The tears running down her cheeks catch in the curves of her smile, dissolving all cares of notice and capture. Ezekiel's heart flutters with wings of elation, realizing that beneath the hows and whys of their matching, he knows why it is meant to be. She is a living symbol of how a flower of light can grow in the darkness. Through her loving kindness, he is freed from a life in which he's only known hardships wrapped in terrifying sadness. He could never pinpoint what it was that drew him to her until this very moment as she tearfully smiles, her eyes speaking the language of the heart.

From the stage, Adramelech continues his speech. "As another way of welcoming the dawn of a new age, and to further mark this joyous occasion, we give you, the people of Zone One, the only friend to the traitor Ezekiel." Adramelech words catch everyone's attention, especially Ezekiel and Lexi's. He points to a massive platform at his left. Slowly rising from beneath it is Cesare. He is chained to a large pillar, his limp body beaten and bloody. "This traitor, this rat, we offer to you, the people. We offer him to you to do with as you please." He turns to Cesare. "Do you have anything to say on your behalf before we unleash these righteous citizens on you?"

Cesare slowly raises his head. "I do. I betrayed my friend not for glory or riches, but for love, for the adoration of the only woman I have ever cared for. She means the world to me. I would sell my life, my dignity, and my friends to protect her from harm and keep her out your grasp."

Lexi, shocked, immediately begins to sob. Serenity holds her firmly by the arms, keeping her from leaping off the stage to be with him.

Cesare goes on. "Citizens of Zone One, I was forced by these monsters to choose between the two people I love most for their own agenda's ends. My friend would understand my reasons for doing so. He is no traitor, nor is he a terrorist. He is one of you, scraping by at the merciless hands of the tyrannical rulers and their governing wolves, who oppress us all for their own gain. He knew that there comes a time when you can't support the machine anymore, when doing so becomes so odious it makes you sick at heart, and you feel the only way to respond is to throw yourself on the wheels, on the gears, on the levers in order to make it stop. He is my brother, and I will always love him as such."

Before he can continue, the Cons beat him into silence. A roar of boos and curses rises up from the crowd, ready to tear him apart.

Iblis scans the crowd to gauge their reaction when he notices Serenity staring at someone, a smile on her lips. He follows her gaze and immediately realizes the source of her unexpected happiness. Lexi, noticing Iblis's dawning realization, begins shaking Serenity, trying to alert her to the danger. Iblis grins a malicious smile before raising the alarm. "He's here! The terrorist has come to finish what he started!" he yells, turning everyone's attention toward Samson and Ezekiel. The crowd immediately draws back from the pair, forming a circle around them.

"Damn, I hate that lizard!" Samson says, covering Ezekiel's back. "We need to leave now. Let's get her and get out of here!"

"No, I can't leave Cesare and Lexi. We have to save them," Ezekiel says, desperation in his voice.

"Fine. But if we don't do it now, there'll be no one to save!"

Cons begin to circle them. "Screw this!" Samson shouts, whipping a mini cannon from under his tattered cloak. He points it into the face of a Con that's reaching for him and without delay begins firing through it onto the rest.

"Slaughter them!" Adramelech screams as Ezekiel charges the stage. Pulling out a sword, he leaps up, only to be stopped by Hiro Mokushiroku, whose gun is pointed at Ezekiel's face. "You've cost us enough!" he says, chambering a round in the pistol. Adramelech orders the Echelon and all surrounding him to seize Ezekiel. Lilith Myriad, the Deracinate president, attempts to grab Serenity but is thrown back when Lexi's tail whips across her face, sending her flying onto Ezekiel's sword. Impaled, Myriad slumps to the stage, distracting Mokushiroku just long enough to allow Ezekiel to flip the sword and plunge it into his heart. Hiro gasps only once before joining Lilith Myriad.

Ravana rushes to Adramelech's side. "Let's get you out of here, sir. I'll initiate the plans." He and a group of Cons hurry the Etharch offstage as the remaining elite flee with the rest of the crowd, who have almost completely dispersed to all sections of the slums.

Serenity rushes to Ezekiel's side. She's about to get lost in his eyes yet again when Lexi's screams break the silence. They turn to look at Iblis, who stands poised over Cesare, ready to deliver a death blow. The creature flashes an evil smile and yells, "You may have stopped the festivities for others, but my pleasures lie in other avenues." He then whispers to Cesare, "Time to finish that inquisition we started a while back."

Before he can act, a powerful blow knocks him off the podium. "That's for sinking my boat!" Samson yells in the middle of fighting Cons.

Returning his attention to his comrade, Ezekiel jumps off the stage, slicing a Con in two. Together, he and Samson fight off the remaining Cons. Lying on the ground, bruised and battered, the two look at each another. Victorious grins are plastered across both of their faces.

"I had them, you know," Samson says, smiling broadly.

"I know. But you wouldn't have left a man alone to defend himself against those odds. Nice shot on that black gecko, by the way."

"Just glad I knocked that smirk off his face," Samson says.

Lexi climbs up to free Cesare. She loosens the chains and wraps him in her arms.

"I…I'm so sorry for…" Cesare struggles to get the words out.

"Don't talk, baby, it's OK. I forgive and I love you." She kisses him deeply.

"Glad he's got his priorities straight," Samson says to Ezekiel as they look on at the two lovers.

"Yes, they deserve to be together," Ezekiel says. "He is right, though. I do understand why he did it. I would have done the same for Serenity." He looks over at her just as she is being hauled away by a limping but still powerful Iblis. "Zeke, help me!" she screams out before being carried up the lift of a hovercraft.

"Great!" Samson shouts, enraged. "What do we do now?"

In a flash, Ezekiel forms a plan. He gives his friend a tracking beacon before hopping on a mach bike parked behind the stage by one of the Cons. "You get Cesare and Lexi out of here before this place is erased. And get in touch with Vanaheim. Let him know they're launching their plans. You can use that beacon to find me later." Samson nods as he steps back, and Ezekiel starts the bike and explodes off in seconds, hidden in a cloud of dust.

Chapter 10

Racing down the streets in his getaway craft, Iblis crushes those caught underneath in the field of his hovercraft's magnetic distribution. Wounded, he drives with his arm and tail, leaving his other arm dangling at his side. Serenity lies unconscious on the floor behind him.

Barreling toward them at the speed of sound, Ezekiel comes up from behind. Iblis notices and quickly drives into the side of a building, sending debris crashing down on Ezekiel and on hordes of screaming onlookers. Ezekiel dodges the falling pieces of wreckage as he speeds toward Iblis, waiting for the opportune moment to make his final strike.

Iblis tries again to finish his pursuer, flooring the engines and ramming again into the side of another building just as Ezekiel uses an abandoned vehicle as a ramp. He flies through the air, jumping off the bike right before Iblis starts shooting straight up. With a crash, Ezekiel lands on the ship.

The force of the landing jolts Serenity awake. She stealthily stands up and jumps on Iblis's back. Reaching from behind, she hits the button on the control panel that opens the hovercraft's doors. Bellowing with rage, Iblis flings her off, allowing Ezekiel the time he needs to enter the vehicle. He lunges at Iblis with all his weight and might, pounding furiously at the creature's flesh. They struggle with one another, locked in a brutal fight as the ship bounces on and off the road. Suddenly, both realize at the same moment that no one is flying the hovercraft. They turn, and a building appears before them. When they crash through the side of the building, the force sends both of them flying through the windshield.

Disoriented and hurt, Iblis laughs while slowly rising to his feet. "Well, I will say this: you're quite entertaining. I wish I could say the same of your friend, though. He didn't put up nearly as much of a fight. I'm truly going to enjoy this." He sends a kick right into Ezekiel's ribcage. "I hope you last longer than your father and don't squeal as your mother did. The sound was quite an annoyance when I burned her from this world." Iblis kicks Ezekiel around the warehouse, which is littered with tools designed for making Cons. The sinister creature peers down at Ezekiel, who now lies still on the unforgiving concrete. Lingering over his prey, Iblis reaches down to finish him when a powerful blow lands across his face, sending him reeling.

Ezekiel rises to his feet, a length of rebar in his hand. "Stick around," he says, spitting blood. "You'll find I'm full of surprises." He throws one hard swing after another, hammering the creature. Iblis's smile fades and his eyes glow red as steam starts to rise from his body.

"Shall we up the stakes a little more?" he hisses, veins of fire bursting through his putrid, soot-colored skin, forming a mist of fire and smoke. His claws start to elongate as spikes grow out of his back, running down the length of his spine and tail. Ezekiel paces carefully around the evil entity, diving and weaving to avoid his sharp, bony claws and the bursts of flames he emits.

"Why are you running?" Iblis asks. "Is my true form too much for you to handle?"

"Not really. You just smell worse now. Like rotten eggs."

The taunt sends Iblis into a rage. He charges forward, slicing at Ezekiel's skin and throwing him across the room with a whip of his tail. "You will never win! This planet is ours! You, your friends, and your kind will all be erased from existence like so many other species we've encountered. To think a creature as feeble as you could destroy the likes of me and the ones I serve is ridiculous."

"I wasn't trying to destroy you. Just buying her enough time." Ezekiel smiles as the creature turns to see Serenity coming up from behind, a fire extinguisher in her hands. She blasts the creature in the face, causing Iblis to writhe in pain. She runs back to the hovercraft as Iblis stands, reverting to his original form and moaning in agony.

"Give us a smile," she says, firing a rocket from the hovercraft and sending Iblis flying into a wall.

She races over to check on Ezekiel. After making sure he's OK, she helps him to his feet. They glance at each other, preparing to leave, when they hear a dying, evil laugh from the corner. They turn as one to see Iblis burning out.

Ezekiel limps over to the remains. "What's so funny?" he asks.

"You've think you've won...in fact, it is I who am the victor. In a minute, what is left of your planet and everything on it will be annihilated. By killing me, all you've done is send one of many back to the plane in which we reside. You think you know who we are? You have no idea." He continues to laugh, coughing up dark, steaming fluids. Ezekiel takes the rebar, a rod of swinging vengeance, in his hands and drives the steel into Iblis's head, silencing his laughter once and for all.

※

"Vanaheim, you have violated our commands and put this whole operation in jeopardy. Now our element of surprise is gone. The Etharchs will make the next move, and we are not fully mobilized yet." The head of the council lets his words hand in the air.

"The attack would have been premature anyway," Vanaheim shoots back. "They would have seen it coming, and we would be in an even worse predicament than we are now. I know what I did was right, and if I am right about what I know, he will not fail us. He will turn the tide in this fight for our survival. He has the key to preventing any more lies from being spread and to stopping the enslavement of our race." Vanaheim stands, his posture exuding the confidence he feels in Ezekiel.

"Captain Nathaniel Vanaheim, you are hereby removed from duty. You will be confined until a tribunal can decide your sentence—if there is still a tribunal left after today!"

Just as Vanaheim is being escorted away, Lexi and Samson burst in, carrying Cesare. "He's right. They were planning to decimate the cities at the very beginning of the festival," Cesare says, his voice dry and weary. "Zeke probably just saved your lives and bought you more time." He looks down in shame. "I should know. I turned him over to them in the first place. As they were torturing me, I overheard them talking. They knew your plans from the very start. They were already prepared to strike with the old bombs first, using your own idea against you. They all laughed about it. They also knew where this place was, which means you have a traitor in your midst."

The council erupts in surprise at this news. "Can you be sure?" "A traitor in our midst, that is impossible!" "How long do we have?"

Their panicked voices subside just long enough for Cesare to grimly deliver his answer. "Any minute now."

The council members begin shouting again. One voice rises above the others. "What do we do now? They have knowledge of all our strategies and will destroy us any minute."

"No, they don't," Samson says, his powerful voice silencing the council members. "They've forgotten Ezekiel. He and Serenity are Skried. If they complete the union, it will disable the whole system, including anything connected through Skrying."

Vanaheim moves to stand at Samson's side. "I am asking this council to have faith and trust as I do. I know Ezekiel will pull this off. We live in a world of a continuous bombardment of regulation made to control us, and directed madness hurrying us to accept the cataclysm they've created. Let us break those chains of mindless servitude and let love rule. The warmth of a heart tempered with grace can light up any space darkened by the cold darkness of fear."

The room is silent for what seems an eternity. At last the council members all nod at each other in agreement. "Very well," Obadiah says. "We will wait and pray our work is not in vain."

"Samson," Vanaheim says, "find Serenity and Ezekiel as quickly as you can. Get them out of the hot zone and back here, pronto."

"I'm on it," Samson replies, moving Cesare into Lexi and Vanaheim's waiting hands. Before he can go, Cesare grabs his arm. "Bring them back," he says. Samson gives a single quick nod and races out of the room.

"I know you'll prove everyone wrong, my boy," Vanaheim says quietly to himself. "I just know it."

Chapter 11

The gears of decimation began to whirl, originating within compartments that house countless Cons and troopers hungry for destruction. Lines of mechanical slayers march in formation, awaiting orders to assault anything standing in their path. The remnants of the vermin elite cling to their alien masters, crawling toward safety from the wrathful fallout soon to be unleashed on the world.

Adramelech barks orders. "Prepare the cargo. Confine and facilitate the fleeing parasites onboard as well. Send out the minions to destroy the puny inhabitants of this rock. Kill them all."

The earth trembles as weapons rise from the ground, as if from black holes deep within the planet itself.

Back at Origen, alarms wail as reports of the Etharchs' mobilization come in.

"What about the missiles?" the council head asks. "Why haven't they launched them yet?"

"They are close to doing so. Five minutes at the most," Vanaheim answers. "First they have to make sure that they'll be able to escape the fallout."

The council head nods gravely. "My fellow council members, it is time to brace for the worst," he says. Captain Vanaheim paces, anxiously waiting for his faith to be vindicated. "Come on, boy," he whispers. "It's all up to you now."

⚏

"Come on, Zeke, it's time to go. It's now or never. Don't die on me!" Serenity pleads with the semiconscious man as she carries him through the streets, looking for a way out of the desolate city. Sirens blare, releasing winds of domination. Frantically looking for any aid, she spots what remains of a vandalized hovercraft, its lifeless owner still inside. Resting Ezekiel on a wall, she runs over to remove the corpse from their only means of escape. She darts back to Ezekiel and drags him into the vehicle. She tries to get it started, but the hovercraft only sputters ineffectually. In frustration she bangs on the gears, which suddenly come to life under her hands. She grabs the steering column and directs the hovercraft straight toward the out-skirts of the city. "We're going to be OK, Zeke. Don't worry. We're going to look back and remember this day as one of victory." She hopes she can keep him awake by talking, as well as hold onto what faith she has left. Through his bleary eyes, he manages to look at her. He reaches out and gently rubs her hand, causing her anxiety to momentarily recede.

They whiz past countless people being pushed and bullied into buildings and homes by emotionless robot soldiers. Serenity's hope for a successful escape rises when she see they are almost out of the city. But before they get there, a flash of light from behind blinds her; she can no longer see the way forward. They look back in hor-ror as she floors it, making a mad dash from the city that is being engulfed by unparalleled destruction. Buildings crumble instantly in fiery infernos, sending shockwaves rippling through the streets. Everything they've known their entire lives is going up in a flash of death. As lives are snuffed out, the Etharchs, having unleashed a bomb on Zone One, enjoy the spectacle from a safe distance.

All eyes are fixed on a screen that shows the ghastly image of missiles launching all over the world. They also see the billowing mushroom cloud that engulfs their own zone.

"That's it, we've lost. All is...lost." The council head drops his head in despair. Cesare and Lexi hold each other tightly as everyone begins to weep and panic—everyone except for Captain Vanaheim, that is. He's still holding out for a miracle.

⁂

"I don't think we're going to make it, Zeke. This may be it." Serenity is pushing the hovercraft to its limits, trying to avoid their certain demise.

Zeke reaches over and grabs her hand. Their eyes meet. "At least we go together," he says quietly. "All death is certain; truly living isn't."

"What are you talking about? We've sacrificed so much to find each other after thinking we would never be able to be together. And now, to be so close to freedom only to lose each other again...it's so..." She trails off, trying to hold back the tears of loss and fear.

"We already have freedom. You gave me freedom when I met you. You brought me to life. No matter what happens next, at least I can say I lived and found happiness in this life. I know now that the Etharchs, your father, the Cons—nobody can take you from me. I've learned that this life isn't all; there's more out there than what is seen with the naked eye. We will always be together."

Ezekiel begins drifting out of consciousness. Serenity forgets to navigate the hovercraft for a moment and simply holds his face in her hands. "Zeke, Zeke, don't go. Stay with me. I feel the same as you do. You showed me what's worth fighting and dying for. You took away my fear. Don't leave me now. I need you. I love you."

Gazing at him, she places her lips on his in an eternal kiss. Her forearm starts to burn, causing her to lean away from him. When she looks down, her neon-blue Skry turns hotter and hotter. Ezekiel's is glowing more brightly too. The sigils begin to pulsate rapidly, unleashing a blinding light from the two as the colors intertwine in a dance above their heads, forming a floating circle that instantly shoots out in all directions. The looming wall of fire behind them vanishes the second the blinding light hits it.

⚌

"Sir, I don't know what just happened, but the explosion—it has disappeared!" an officer exclaims to the Origen council.

"What are you talking about? How can sheer annihilation just vanish?" the council head asks.

"I don't know, but all the bombs are falling out of the sky, almost as if…"

"They were taken off-line." Captain Vanaheim says in astonishment. "The union—they did it. Anything tied to the Etharchs by way of being Skried is shutting down." Some of the machines in Origen's own facility abruptly die and go off-line. "He did it."

⚌

The hovercraft shuts down in midair, gliding only on the wind underneath it. As it begins to go into a slight nosedive, Serenity grabs Ezekiel, holding him tight. "I'll see you on the other side," she says, closing her eyes and kissing his hand. The craft plummets into a field, skidding several yards before flipping over and rolling until it stops. The engine hisses its final breath before fading out. Smoke rises from the silence all around as death's voice commands all sound. Ashes dance within pillars of smoke rising from the city.

On the ground just beyond the borders of the city, outside the downed craft, Ezekiel and Serenity hold each other. Within moments, the Skries on their forearms gently disappear.

Chapter 12

Thunderous cheers of victory fill the air. Nothing but relieved and happy faces abound as Origen puts the Etharchs and their minions on notice. Cesare looks down at his forearm to see his Skry has vanished. Looking over at Lexi, he starts weeping tears of joy, realizing now that nothing can or will ever stop them from being together. They lock in tight embrace, kissing and laughing as members of the council jump and dance with the other citizens of their underground home. Captain Vanaheim wears a quiet, satisfied smile, knowing his faith didn't let him down. He knew the father and the son, and had full confidence in the ability of both to disprove the naysayers and the disingenuous about the existence of miracles. He doesn't know if Ezekiel is alive or not. The one thing he truly knows and accepts is the knowledge that everything will change from here on.

He also knows the Etharchs will want retribution for their failure, and that Castiel's son, a kindred spirit and new friend, may have just handed them the deciding word on who rules whom on Earth. The balance of power has begun to shift away from those selfishly claiming all for themselves. The devastating mechanical armies have started to turn off, along with anything else connected to the Skry sigils. Cities, factories, and buildings begin to go black and dead in a rippling wave of technological shutdown across the world. Human soldiers controlled through nervous-system monitoring begin to go off-line, permanently. High above the earth, the elite and their kind scream in agony and terror as Etharchs tear each one asunder piece by piece.

Adramelech stares down at Earth, his expression inscrutable. He knows his superiors will be displeased on learning what has happened. They will take over his command immediately, forcing him to plead for his position among those living in limbo. At his side, Ravana mulls over his own fate as the mutilation and murder of his fellow elites rages behind him.

⚏

Eyes of blue light stare off into the distance, piercing the haze before a rumbling sound approaches, then disappears. Lights emerge from the fog only to fade away. Footsteps crunch on the ground, breaking the silence. The wind begins to whistle, blowing the mist away and revealing the downed hovercraft.

Samson rushes to the vehicle's smoking remains. When he gets there, he sees Ezekiel and Serenity's motionless bodies in the front, locked in eternal embrace. He stumbles to his knees in grief just as Ezekiel opens his eyes.

"Thought you were dead!" Samson says to him in happy disbelief.

"I've seen enough horror in my time. Didn't know you felt that way for me."

Samson chuckles. "You're biased. Before you met her, I was the prettiest thing around."

Ezekiel begins to laugh until a fit of coughing stops him. Flecks of blood dot his mouth. He glances at his beauty, pale and cold to the touch in his arms. He brushes the hair away from her face, noticing for the first time that her sigil is gone. He looks down to see that his is gone too. "We did it? We shut the system down?"

"Yeah, everything attached to the Skrying system has been rendered ineffective. You should see all the giant new paperweights they have back at Origen," Samson says.

"I think I'll just take your word for it, my friend."

"I know. You should also know that Cesare and Lexi are safe, and you stopped all the missiles. Apparently the Etharchs had them connected to the Skrying system. When you shut it off, they all fell out off the sky like rocks. Most of the Cons were also disrupted and disconnected, as well as the Watcher system. You saved us, man."

"The battle is all we have won. There is something coming that's even more terrifying, and it's not just a feeling I have. I've seen things that even in this world are too hard to imagine. All I can say is that Origen's going to need you now more than ever, Samson. Something far worse than the Etharchs is looming on the horizon. Carry on, my friend. Carry on the good fight. I'm going to my lady. Don't join us too soon." Ezekiel smiles before closing his eyes, leaving only the grin on his face.

"Don't worry," Samson whispers. "I won't let you down, bro." He places Ezekiel's hands back on his love and says to himself, "Who would have thought one kiss could do all this?" Samson stands up to retrieve his battered vehicle. He's going to bring his friend and the girl who changed his life back to Origen headquarters for a proper burial. But before he takes another step, he notices light swelling around their bodies. Brilliant beams of neon blue and cerulean rise into the heavens, twirling around each other and dancing into the sky.

Samson smiles, knowing they are truly at peace now. He continues to watch as lights pick up their pace. At last they flash into the stars before getting lost among them, away from all the violence and indifference infecting the living, bound for true peace among happiness and light.

Samson retrieves his vehicle. He gently picks them up, bringing them to the vehicle. It's time to regroup with the others. He isn't a clairvoyant and doesn't know what Ezekiel meant about something coming, but it doesn't take a diviner of realms to know this is just the beginning. The fires of revolution will rage, truth will soon expose all, and flocks of helpless people will rally to the cause of freedom. Nevertheless, those who want to ensnare the less fortunate won't disappear entirely. They will still eat the weak and drink their fear, harboring cruel and heinous thoughts in their endless pursuit of power.

But no matter what lies on the horizon, he will be ready. He won't go quietly into the abyss. He remembers something he was told as a young man: "Keeping a balance between passion in the heart and reason in the mind will never lead you astray. Frail deeds hold not here and now, with the odds stacked against us. Yet even blind eyes can blaze like meteors against the sun and dying light. Liberation of the mind from the restraints of social injustice lights rebellious fires and fierce tears. When a brave man takes a stand, the spines of others are often stiffened."

Samson knows a time of retribution is coming, a time to punish those responsible for the destruction of their word, to make a stand against those who would terminate the very idea of freedom. The war has just begun.